Another

AT THE

TABLE

Another
AT THE
TABLE

**A SURFSIDE BEACH
NOVELLA**

KELLY CAPRIOTTI BURTON

Published by Kelly Capriotti Burton
Cover design by Kelly Capriotti Burton

ISBN: 9798781402977
ISBN EBook: 9781736117446

Kellofastory.com
Surfside Beach, South Carolina

For the siblings:

· the one I grew up with.

· the gathered ones, with whom I'll grow old.

· my favorite set: Josh, Paige, Miranda, Kaity, Jack, & Kirsten (& Nora, too), for always welcoming another at the table.

[1]

"What are you looking at?" she said. The swirl-scrub-swirl motion she was making in the bottom of the slow cooker had captured all of her concentration, but Jessie was able to feel Paul's green-eyed stare from a room away. Right then, he was sitting at the kitchen table, only feet from her, and when she turned to look back, he was smiling that smile.

"Seriously? What?" She peeled off her gloves and wiped at her forehead. Who needed cardio when you could just clean up after a hearty chowder? Blast Amazon Prime for not delivering the Crock Pot liners even though she'd forgotten to actually reorder them. Blast Alexa for not growing robotic arms and keeping the bottom of the pot from burning.

She would let it soak, Jessie decided, and turned around to face her fiancé.

"I was just wondering if you could go change into those special, um, pants, you wore to Summer's school yesterday."

She rolled her eyes, walking to him, letting him put his hands on her hips as he accepted the inevitable admonishment. "The Santa leggings? Those are for Storytime with Mimi only."

Paul lifted her hand to his lips and kissed it so softly she almost couldn't feel it. "Will you tell me a story then?"

Ah, yes. "Once upon a time," she murmured with a smile, "There was a woman who was all alone. For like 36 seconds. And then her friend kissed her, turned into a prince, and they lived happily ever after."

He stood then, still staring at Jessie in the intense way he had that was familiar and unnerving all at once. "It's a good story," he said softly.

She couldn't help it. Her heart still beat a little faster when he was so close and so intent.

...

It shouldn't have surprised her to feel the butterflies. They'd packed more changes than she could list into a few months, really, and everything felt new. Every single day held another new thing. She'd long rolled her eyes at the term "new normal," but since an accident in the early spring had claimed the lives of both her and Paul's spouses, since she and her once co-worker had found life to be short and love again to be worth a risk, since a thousand other pieces of her life that existed at the beginning of that year had changed completely, she had to concede that her normal was really new, and also, she couldn't quite manage to consider it normal yet.

But there was Paul. He'd become her anchor, her anchor who could stare at her in the quiet of the morning, over coffee on their patio or sitting on the beach, across a room of their somewhat-blended and very noisy brood, and make her melt no matter what the circumstance. And, there was possibly about to be a circumstance.

"Maybe I'll go change real quick," she murmured, enjoying the feel of his arms around her waist.

"Mmm," he answered. "Santa leggings?"

"Well, yes. It might help soften the blow."

His hands did not drop from her waist, but they did tighten their grip. He knew her tone so well.

"Aw Jess. What? Please don't tell me we have to go hunt for our own Christmas turkey or make gluten free lasagna noodles from scratch or something."

She giggled. Paul's patience with her culinary adventures had run out around the time he waited over an hour for her to finish a seven layer cake before, ahem, commencing to the bedroom. Specifically, he told her he'd rather eat Food Lion brand Oreos for every dessert for the rest of his life than watch her prepare and clean that mess when they could be "relaxing" in bed.

"It has nothing to do with food; I promise." Then she hesitated, caressing his arm. "Well, unless the quantity of food counts. Because it will involve... more... food."

"FFS," he muttered. It had become his favorite acronym since Jacob, her six-year-old grandson, had exclaimed the actual words it stood for during a spirited game of Sorry on one now-infamous Taco Tuesday. Jacob's daddy, Jessie's oldest son Sam, had made them all a bit sorry in the aftermath.

"Why, Jess? Who besides our one-million-family-members-minus-one-hostile-daughter is going to be here for our first Christmas?"

His voice trailed off. She was not surprised to hear hints of frustration in his voice, but mostly what she noted was the veiled sadness. And that added to her sadness. It was going to be such a weird holiday, to say the least. It would be the first without Randall, Jessie's husband of 36 years and beloved daddy of their four kids. It would be the first without

Leah, Paul's wife of 33 years and mother of their three daughters.

And it would be the first of Jessie and Paul together, because everything happened at breakneck speed. Ugh. She grimaced. It had been a terrible car accident following Randall's massive coronary that had started the whole sequence of events.

"Just Maggie," Jessie answered, but she let it imply the wider spectrum that was held in her best friend's name.

"Just Maggie? Not her brand-new husband? Not any of their big, fat, non-Greek, newly blending family?"

"Oh, Paul…"

At that, he removed his hands from Jessie and took a few steps… away. The break in contact was already such a clear signal between them. He was going to be exasperated, and she was going to have to give him a minute.

She held her words. Instead of trying to explain, she moved to the counter and wiped it aggressively. Then she started brewing a half pot of decaf. And then, she felt him inches behind her. When she turned, his mouth was still held in a stressed line, but his green eyes were twinkling at her. The butterflies fluttered their wings.

"Sheldon and all the kids, too," Jessie said quietly. "They're not staying with us—"

"I mean, we'd have to move out if they did!"

It wasn't true. Their charming and deniably eclectic beach cottage had two guest bedrooms (three if you counted the "cousin sleepover bunk bed nook" just off the laundry room), plus a small, private in-law suite. Maggie and her husband and their combined four adult kids (okay, and one tiny little grandson) could easily fit physically into their home for a few days, even with Jessie's youngest son David coming for a stay.

Could they fit into the carefully balanced, a little bit

tenuous feeling of home Jessie and Paul were still creating? If Jessie paused for a moment and was honest with herself – admittedly, somewhat shamefully, kind of a brand-new phenomenon at her AARP age, it was too much. Maggie was a bundle of energy, like a tornado dressed in a fabulous boho maxi-dress with shimmering sandals, and Maggie and Jessie together could not contain themselves. And Maggie and Jessie together when they now lived four hours apart? Probably for a day or two, it could feel like the world only held the two of them. There would be wine and cheese spreads, lists of discussion topics, at least one re-watch of something Julia Roberts starred in when her hair was big and fabulous. There would be laughter, random kids joining in, spontaneous outings to this store or that café.

When she thought about it, saw it through Paul's eyes, saw it through her widow-living-a-new-chapter-and-discovering-her-new-damn-normal-self eyes, it seemed like a lot. It almost seemed overwhelming.

She missed Maggie so much she had to refrain from thinking about her some days. The absence of her soul sister in her day-to-day life left an ache that honestly was right behind missing Randall, her mother, and her dog Cash, whose strong Labrador tail she could still hear thumping against her furniture even though he'd been gone for 84 days.

But Maggie had somehow been relegated to the before. Before Randall died. Before Paul moved in. Before Jessie and Paul broke up. Before Jessie lost her dog, sold her house, and got a little skinny. Before she and Paul reconciled, bought a new house together, and got engaged, in spite of what seemed like a billion complications and potential obstacles. Maggie was already married and living in Greenville when Jessie's current new had started. What would it be like now? How would Paul factor in? Would Maggie act the same? Would Jessie be the same?

"Jess!"

She realized that Paul had said her name a few times while she contemplated the cosmos that was their union. She half-smiled, half-grimaced at him. She knew what was coming next.

"It's not that big of a deal," Paul said, reaching for her hand, because it seemed that although he didn't share her touchy-feely-ness, or what her daughter Brittney called her "cutesy little heart," he always seemed to want to be touching Jessie. She didn't mind; if the physical link calmed him, it reassured her to no end. She wished she didn't need it, but... sigh. Everything was new!

"You know how I feel about Maggie," he said evenly. And Jessie did. Paul had known Maggie for years, first just through Jessie's own steady stream of stories during their work days, and then through the companionship their families enjoyed. Anyway, of course he liked Maggie. Everyone liked Maggie.

"I also know how you feel about the chaos."

"Just tell me what the plan is, Jess. I'm not made of glass..."

"She and the girls are going to stay here for two nights . When Sheldon, Eddy, Maya, and the baby get here, the day before Christmas Eve, they're renting a house. It overlaps one night with David's arrival, and probably with Katy's, but David can sleep on the couch or crash with Sam or Brit for a night..."

"There's plenty of room for all of the kids here, Jess." Paul's deadpan tone was betrayed by his hands, as he slipped them deftly back to her hips, clad not in Santa loungewear but, frankly, a very curve-hugging pair of jeans.

"The kids?"

"Yep." He kissed her neck and let his face linger there. She felt his lips curve into a smile. "Plenty of space for all of them. But you and Mags? You're going to have to get a room."

[2]

"**M**oni, I am not asking Auntie Jess to put up with any more of us! Not another person, not another day. It is what it is. Tell him to get a hotel room or wait and see you after Christmas."

I didn't know what this child was thinking. And yes, I knew good and flippin' well that she wasn't a child. She was a grown-tail woman. But, when you go from a house of three ladies all your life to a new husband, new boyfriend, stepsiblings, nephew, and all the things, it starts getting a little crazy.

So here is Moni – after I have sprung our visit on Jessie, telling me she wants to bring a guy she's been dating for three months. I can't even keep a handle on his name. Trez? Ted? Ty? No idea. Three months? Please. I'll be surprised if they make it to Christmas, much less that I'll want to see him in family pictures of this big ol' important holiday for the rest of our lives.

So Moni sighed, and came just short of stomping her 27-year-old feet, but she nodded her head and walked away. I guess to the patio. Or the bathroom. She didn't live here; Sheldon and I did, and his son Eddie. Moni had had her own place for a few years, well before I moved away from the beach to Charlotte.

And now I sat at the table, my kitchen table, the one I shared with my new husband. I really, really, really could not believe that my best friend, my sister-in-law, well, my sister really... that she and I had both fallen in love this year.

In fact if I looked back on the past year, I could never have predicted that anyone but she and Randall would have been at my wedding. In fact, I probably would have had Randall give me away. He was the closest thing to a brother I would ever have in my life. He was a little bit of a father figure to me. I mean, my own father died right before I married Tony and when Jessie's no-good brother left the girls and me so many years ago, Randall came and collected us. Packed the moving truck. Drove the moving truck. Let us stay in his already chaotic house until we found ours. Thank God it only took about a week and a half, back when housing in Myrtle Beach wasn't completely stupid, when the entire northeast wasn't retiring to "planned communities," and I was able to get a well-lit apartment near Jess and Randall until I bought a house the next year, a five-minute drive to the beach and a huge oak tree shading the backyard.

He was always there for us. Fixing things for us. Getting my oil changed. Taking the girls to daddy-daughter dances. He was the best, and my heart was left in a thousand pieces when he died, just like everyone else's. And I kind of wanted to strangle Jess when three weeks later, she started dating Paul. How can you start dating three weeks after your husband of 36 years dies suddenly? How can you start dating one of your husband's best buddies three weeks later? But the fact of the matter was, who was I to talk? I'd been alone so many years after Tony left. Sure I had dates. I had flings. I had things. But none of them filled or even touched that empty part of life that only a husband, a partner, could fill.

So I couldn't blame her. I couldn't begrudge her because she happened to find the empty-place-filler, well, about 20 years sooner than I had.

Anyway. Right after she started dating Paul, I met Sheldon. And that happened plenty fast, too… faster than I ever imagined that it would, or it could, or I wanted it to happen. But he was perfect for me. He filled my space. So he also made it easier for me to forgive Jessie. No. Not forgive. She didn't do a thing to me. My timing with Sheldon made it easier for me to understand Jessie's timing with Paul. And that helped me completely, without a doubt, embrace my role as the one who would help her kids understand.

Oh, things looked mostly fine now, but there were conversations she knew nothing about. Every single one of those children called me, asking me what their mama was thinkin', what was she doing, could I talk her down, could I stop her, could I change it. And I always told them, No. Not only could I not, I wouldn't if I could. But I told them with an auntie's love, and let's face it, there's nothing like that.

It was the same way Jessie loved my girls, and I knew she would never say no to Moni bringing her boyfriend to her house (her new house, in which she'd barely finished hanging just the right pictures for a blended life or wrinkling the sheets with her soon-to-be new husband). But I wasn't going to ask. Even though she and Paul were reconciled, and things were happy, and they were starting to talk about a wedding, I just wasn't going to throw that on her. To be truthful, I wasn't going to spring it on Paul. God bless him. He was used to a much quieter life with Leah. He was never going to have that with Jessie, not with the way she lived, like the old woman in the shoe... so many kids, she didn't know what to do... and always, always, always opening the door to one more. That's just who Jessie is. And those of us who were blessed to be in her inner circle, we had to accept it. We had to accept that there was always gonna be some surprise guest at the weekly supper or the girls' night out, Thanksgiving dinner or Christmas Eve, and just because Randall was gone, that was not going to change. Paul was going to have to live with it, too.

As for me and my house, we missed it. My girls and Jessie's kids were first cousins. They spent their adolescent and teen years around the same tables, in the same noisy holidays. And my girls had never had an up-close example of what a relationship should look like, save for Jess and Randall, and that was over and gone. I was sure gonna try to play catch-up with Sheldon, and I really wanted this to be a holly, jolly Christmas.

"Moni," I called. "Now."

When she re-appeared I said, "Why don't you call your cousin Sam and see if Trey can stay there for a few nights?"

"Mama, that's so weird. Trey barely knows you. He's going to go stay with Sam and Abby?"

"Babe, take it or leave it. I don't care if he comes or not, but I would like to avoid your face being long as the Sears Tower during the roast beast."

"It's the Willis Tower now, Mama." She smiled at me, just a little, through her protests. Whatever it was called, I didn't want to see more disappointment on Christmas than we had to, and there would be plenty. I wanted it to be a simple, joyous day at the end of the one of the hardest and downright weirdest years ever.

[3]

"David, just get here. We haven't seen you in months. I don't understand the dawdling."

"Yeah, David. Quit being a bit titty baby and get your ass in the car!"

"Brittney, not helpful. Oh, for crying out loud. Summer, hand Mimi a towel, please."

"Ew! Is that throw up?"

Jessie turned from her son's face on the kitchen iMac screen and toward her grandson Jacob's disgusted scowl, inches away from her granddaughter Josie, now the ripe age of seven weeks and away from her mama, Jessie's oldest daughter Mikayla, for the first evening ever.

"Jacob, go find something to do. Summer, hurry, please."

Breastfed Josie wasn't much of a puker, but Jessie suspected the break in her comfortable routine, which was basically in her mama or daddy's arms, had stressed out the little pumpkin pie. The surrounding noise was enough to cause anyone nausea anyway; Josie's older cousins were naturally loud, there was palpable tension between Jessie and David, even over Facetime , and that was punctuated by the peanut gallery also known as Brittney, the baby of Jessie's brood until David came along. One would never know they were in their 20s from their choices in name-calling toward each other.

Jessie gently swabbed Josie's tiny mouth, then more vigorously scrubbed the trail of ick down her own bare arm. Baby puke really didn't phase her, but David always did, and she was getting a hot flash, sitting in a tank top, in mid-December, listening to him make excuses for skipping Christmas, their first Christmas without Randall.

"Julie isn't coming, David!" Brittney popped her head right next to Jessie's and into view, and in the little inset window at the bottom of the screen, Jessie could see her scowl. Steel yourself, she wanted to tell baby Josie. Your Auntie Brit is about to explode. "We all know that all this nonsense about your little job and promising Uncle Joel you would help tile a shower is just crap. So pack your stuff, wash your hair, put on some decent shoes, and get here to spend Christmas with everyone, David!"

"Mom—" was David's response. At that precise moment, a runaway Nerf bullet came flying across the room, hit Josie on her nose, probably didn't hurt but made her cry, and Summer started screaming at Jacob. Oh, and Jessie's phone was ringing.

"I will call you back later tonight, love." Jessie blew David a quick kiss and tapped the red "end" button. Josie appeared only to be offended, not injured, but Brittney was ranting as Summer beat Jacob with a pillow.

"I'm sure there is an errand somewhere I forgot to run…"

The sardonic voice of Paul startled her through the chaotic din. Before she could say a word, he put two fingers to his mouth and sent out a shrieking whistle. Everyone was silent, except for Josie, who reacted with a brand-new sound that seemed between a surprised giggle and a terrified whimper.

"Poppy P!" Jacob charged Paul, who caught him in some kind of wrestling hold before his head hammered Paul's ribs.

"Little man. Chill a moment." Jessie couldn't help but smile at his Principal Paul voice. It was almost the same as his Poppy P voice. The whistle was new, though… and probably totally necessary.

Paul seamlessly scooped the baby from her arms with the hand not holding Jacob, making Jessie swoon a little like a teenager. He kissed Josie's head and let Jacob go, saying, "Stay right there, sir."

"Hey Brit, can you and Summer go grab some food? Chipotle? Chicken? Chinese? Any of the "c" groups. Cookies. I don't care. Here—" He handed Brittney a few bills and the smoke rising from her ears over her brother turned to charmed acquiescence at her almost-stepdad's chivalry.

"We'll be back soon. Come on, Summer."

Summer gave Jacob one more glare before taking Brittney's lead. Paul called after her to get lots of sweet tea, from anywhere, and then he walked Jacob into the cousin nook. Jessie heard a sustained low murmur, then the TV flipped on, then her fiancé strolled back into the kitchen smiling widely first at her, then back down at Josie. Their grandbaby, she thought. Josie would never know Randall. Paul would be her Poppy. Paul would soon be Jessie's second husband, this wonderful, charming, capable man who wanted to take care of her and loved her family and admired her legs in silly holiday wear. What did she do to be so blessed again? And simultaneously, how she wished Randall could know their first-born's first-born.

"What in the bless-ed world is going on?" Paul teased, handing Josie back.

"It was supposed to be Taco Tuesday evening," she shrugged. "With the added bonus of infant separation anxiety and David and Brittney having a battle royale."

"What now?"

"He doesn't want to come home for Christmas. Says he promised Joel he would help him do a quick remodel on their bathroom before the spring semester starts…"

"But he really is just avoiding Julie?" Paul asked, deadpan.

Jessie sighed. David and Paul's daughter Julie, slightly older, way more grown up than David, had decided they were in love around the same time Jessie and Paul had. Julie had also decided she completely disapproved of her father's new relationship and that David dropping out of USC and moving to Arizona with her to become midwives was a smart idea. It had lasted mere weeks. She broke up with him for a doctor; he tucked his tail and settled in Tennessee, near Randall's sister.

Jessie and Paul's relationship nearly didn't survive it, and what followed their break-up were the eight loneliest weeks of Jessie's life. Even now, reconciled and living in their new home, the subject of Paul's somewhat estranged daughter always brought some tension. At least Jessie didn't have to fix her face at the mention of Julie's name anymore. She's going to be my daughter, she would repeat to herself. Oh, she knew that Julie was likely to even reject the notion of stepdaughter for years to come, but Jessie took her cues from Randall, (who never, ever called himself Sam's stepfather, even before the adoption), and from her own heart. She gathered people and made them her people. And even though the thought of Julie's behavior toward David, toward her, toward Paul, still made her involuntarily twitch and inwardly cuss, she hoped one day, by some miracle, all of that would come to peace, and she could gather Julie, too.

She hadn't answered Paul and didn't need to. "At least he's enrolled in school," Paul continued.

"At least," she said wryly. "I realize the irony of it. A few months ago I couldn't imagine being sad over him making responsible, adult decisions. But it's Christmas. I just want him home. It's—"

She couldn't finish and didn't have to. One of their biggest struggles, especially right now with all the holiday madness, was how to honor. How could they honor their kids? Their memories? Each other? Themselves?

Jessie could figure most of it out. But she struggled with that last one. It was December 16, and each of the next 15 days had at least one event on her calendar.

"How's the calendar looking?"

Paul could read her mind. She was more certain of it every single day.

Laughing, but inwardly cringing, she shoved her planner across the table at him. The sound jostled baby Josie. Jessie stroked her cheek and thought it would be nice just to do that for two weeks, sit in her kitchen with Paul and love the baby.

He glanced through a few of her color-coded pages, neat little notes, heart-shaped bullet points, and exclamatory scrawls across much of their surface, and grimaced.

"Don't say it," she murmured.

"When will you breathe, Jess? I know your kids and the little ones are going to be full of the feelings. But so will you…"

Jessie looked down at Josie, her little lips puckering for the milk in her dreams, and sighed. "I know. I will. I… I don't know where to start. I thought I was starting with family, and planning the things with everyone, and I could just fill myself in around all of that. I mean, one of those days is filled with a spa appointment…"

"With Maggie!" Paul laughed. "That's about as peaceful as a fire alarm in the middle of the night."

She couldn't argue. "Okay. So I will walk on the beach by myself. Every day. Which is not different from any other day. But I will walk with intention." The intention of mourning…

Paul didn't answer. There wasn't much else he could say. He always wanted Jessie to take better care of herself than she did. She always waved off his concern a bit. He wasn't a mama. His family was smaller. He was an introvert. He didn't understand all the commotion that she welcomed. He didn't understand that homemade Italian Christmas cookies, the ones with anise and multi-colored non-perils, could not just be picked up at Costco or even the magnificent Trestle Bakery out in Conway and be the same thing.

Yeah. She heard herself in her head. Some of her priorities were possibly bordering the absurd at times.

"I will breathe," she said. "And I promise not to get too angry when you have to remind me…"

"Inhale," he said pointedly, his smile melting her insides. She did. "Now exhale." She obeyed again. "Now tell me what you need."

"I need to know that you're okay…" she started.

He nodded. "I am. And I will be. I think… I think Christmas Eve will be the toughest day. That was Leah's big day, big fancy brunch with her sisters. Movie and appetizers with the girls after church. They even did the matching pajamas. And I can't duplicate that for them—before you say it, I couldn't even if you and I weren't together, Jess. It was all Leah's thing. I was a spectator."

She could picture it in her mind. Paul was a hands-on dad

to his daughters, but he and Leah didn't exactly do the thing together. Paul did the homework help, the college tours, the golf lessons, the homecoming games. Leah took them shopping and away on weekends, they ran races together, tried new restaurants, curated looks, had Netflix marathons. All together? There were a few things, but if Jessie looked back with the filter of Paul's commentary, she could see their lives were a little separate. What she didn't know was how he felt about it.

"So… what did you do while they watched their movie and ate their froo-froo food? It doesn't sound like Randall's cup of tea, either." If she mentioned Randall, sometimes it made it easier for Paul to mention Leah.

"Oh, I was there. They usually made me something that wasn't over-the-top, like pigs in a blanket with fancy ketchup." He smiled almost sheepishly. "And I usually baked cookies, just from the refrigerated dough, and I put them out for Santa. And I ate one or two of them once the girls were over Santa."

She smiled with him. That part of the memory, she had heard before, but picturing it now hit differently. Jessie would never get used to the odd mingle of sweetness and sadness that every family memory seemed to hold.

"Maybe…"

"It's not like Danielle will be here either," Paul said, reading her mind again. "So if there is any re-creating, it will likely be Katy and me eating cookie dough straight from the tub. But I want to spend the evening with you, too, Jess. And all the other kids. And the grandkids who will be here. I really do."

"You could do it with Christian," she suggested. Paul's grandson was four and would be thrilled to leave cookies and reindeer food out at his Poppy's house.

"He'll be doing that at his house, Jess." He squeezed her

hand.

"It's fine. You're fine. We're fine. Everything is fine," she said, shaking her head, smirking. They should have shirts printed up with that phrase on one side and "new (friggen) normal" on the other.

"It's going to be so different." Jessie knew it was one of the dumbest things she'd ever said, but she really didn't have another word. She surmised most people in mourning had a first year of only the honoring and the grief to get through. She and Paul added at least two extra layers of complication. Would the sheer volume and madness of so many people make the sorrow more bearable, or would it just be too loud, too much?

"I think I'll ask if Danielle and Katy want to do something together the night before Christmas Eve," Paul said.

Jessie smiled at him. "I think that's a great idea." She and her kids, minus David, apparently, were going to gather at Sam and Abby's that same evening.

The truth was, she wanted to be with Paul every second of the holiday.

And she wanted to be in a little bubble with all her grown babies and the not-grown ones and maybe Maggie and just bask in the crappiness of a Christmas without Randall, their rock.

And she wanted to be alone and feel everything and cry when she wanted or not at all.

And in that moment, she let herself admit, she would probably trade all her present joys and future dreams to have her husband back with them for just one more Christmas.

[4]

"**Y**ou all packed then, sunshine?"
I gave my husband my biggest, most unreserved smile. He deserved it, calling me a nickname like that. He'd sing the songs to go along with it, too. *Ain't no sunshine when she's gone. I got sunshine on a cloudy day.* Even, *You are my sunshine, my only sunshine.*

I offered him my cheek. Sheldon brushed it with his lips, then moved them to my neck and lingered. I sighed. Suddenly, I didn't want to go.

"I wish you could leave with me," I said, returning his kisses.

"Mmm," he said. "So do I... but it's only a few days. And you and Sissy will need the time just to catch up."

Sissy. Sheldon had a twin sister of his own, Carla, who lived in Puerto Rico and whom he missed dearly, and whom he called "Sissy." I never even referred to Jessie as *Sissy*, but Sheldon had before he even met her.

(Pause…just to love my life!)

"We do," I agreed, never breaking physical contact with him. He towered over me by six inches. His coffee-colored eyes were intense and playful all at once, and he smelled like musk and leather and my greatest dream come true. The only *other* thing that could ever make me pause on my way to see my *sissy* was Sheldon.

He gave me a swift, powerful hug and pulled himself away to fetch his breakfast. He'd already gone to the gym, downed his protein shake, showered. That was 300% more activity than I liked before 8am. I was more the put-on-robe, run-diffuser, drink-three-coffees, read-one-chapter, scroll-mindlessly-for-20-45-minutes type. And now that I was packed, I would scroll for another minute. I was spying Paul's daughter Julie a bit, for Jessie, of course, because she'd been blocked. There was typically not much "public," (I obviously couldn't be her *Friend*) outside of the occasional churchy video or birth-related news feature. And there wasn't anything today. But there on the spawned-from-hell Facebook messenger, there was something else… the only other thing that could make me hesitate on my way to visit my sister.

"Message requests" was lit up with that little red notification flag. And when I clicked on it, as I did once a week or so, expecting to see spam or a leftover dreg from my online dating days, I saw a name that had been absent from the printed *or* digital portions of my life since the divorce papers were signed, almost 20 years before.

Anthony T. Romano. *Anthony?* Since when had Tony gone by the full, given name that he'd abhorred? Was this really him or some kind of joke? Should I tap or leave it sitting there? Should I call Jessie immediately or never tell her?. Oh my Lord. *Oh my Lord.*

I tapped. Of course I did. And it was really him. Of course

it was.

Why? Why now?

I looked at my ex-husband's profile picture before I read his words. He didn't look the same. Why would he? In the grand scheme, he was basically a child when he moved away, a little scrawny and struggling to grow a full mustache, because at the time that was all firefighters were allowed. And now he was… filled out. Not overweight, exactly, but not 30 and 150 pounds anymore either. He had a salted dark goatee and a very small smile that didn't quite reach his blue eyes. His head was shaved, *shaved.* Just like Sheldon's. But so different.

I snooped around his profile. It gave nothing away. His occupation was listed as Administration at Mesa Fire Department. Well. That explained the facial hair. He wasn't facing the public anymore. But I couldn't tell what the heck else he might be doing. There were no signs of relationship status, friends, hobbies, places he liked, and certainly not that he had two grown daughters who lived across the country.

He'd been out of my system for years, but I felt my blood start its slow, raging simmer. I took a deep breath, closed his profile, and tapped that message.

Maggie. It's really you, right? I want to be sure before I say much else. It is Tony… your daughters' father. I suppose it doesn't sit well with you that I call myself that, but I just wanted you to know it's really me. If you would rather use email than this, it's below. It would be good to hear from you.

"It would be good to hear from you?" Who the blazes does he think he is? *"Your daughters' father?"* The hell you are. Baby-daddy ain't even a term for you. Sperm-donor. Bottom-feeder. Half-man who gave me the only two, microscopic bits of himself that were worth anything.

Randall was more of a father to Nora and Moni. Sheldon was more. Morgan Freeman narrating *March of the Penguins* was more.

I did not reply. I swiped and tapped delete. And then I went back to his profile and blocked his ass. A small voice inside me (it sounded a little like Nora when she was trying to boss me) reminded me that it was Christmas. Jesus went from a little miracle baby to a God-man who audibly forgave the people who tortured and crucified him.

"Hush," I said out loud. I didn't have the patience for the Holy Ghost or the time for ghosts of Christmas past. My sissy was waiting.

[5]

"**M**aggieeeeeeeeeeeeee!"

My best friend's voice was better than the jingliest of bells. Nora and Moni just laughed as I threw off my seatbelt like I was pulling a parachute cord. I ran up the driveway and embraced Jessie as fiercely as I could.

"Sister. I can't believe how long it's been." She tightened her hold for just a moment before letting go. She knew my tolerance for long hugs was much less than hers.

"Me either," I said, stepping back to take her in.

"I mean, I guess it's only been a month, but it feels like forever. I'm so used to you living down the flippin' street."

"I know. I know…" I thought of Sheldon's warm smiles as I left the house that morning and how his kiss felt right before I got in the car, as my girls politely and bemusedly looked away. I loved him. I loved being married to him. But my Lord, did I miss my Jessie.

"Girls!" Jessie called out in her Chicago accent with just a hint of twang. She was like half sweet, half unsweet tea... didn't really make sense but you couldn't help but love it once in awhile, especially when your sugar was way too high.

Nora and Moni let themselves be hugged and kissed and fawned over, and then they retrieved the bags from the car because they knew there was no way I was going to spend time on such menial tasks.

Jessie has already set up shop on her new front porch, which wasn't anything like her old front porch. That one had been cavernous and faced the beach. This one faced the road, but it was a sweet road, as everything "east of 17" (that is, beachfront) in Surfside was sweet. I had lived there myself, just a mile and a half from Jessie. I was near the library and Fuller Park, the tennis court and the weekly Farmer's Market, in a two-bedroom house from when that still existed, with a willow tree and tire swing in the front yard. I thought I would live there forever, even after Nora and Moni stayed upstate after college. I thought I'd have grandbabies buying Jupiter Pies with me at the market and floating on that swing. But Sheldon changed everything, and his law firm would be much harder to move than my banking job was to resign.

So I settled in with Jessie on a piece of her new life. Paul was much more of an outdoorsman that Randall (I'm sorry, but I'm gonna compare, okay?), so there were flowers everywhere even though it was almost Christmas. Of course there were twinkling lights plus one of those silhouetted wooden nativity scenes plus little solar lanterns lining the sidewalk. It honestly looked magical.

I was happy for them.

"How you doin', kid?" I asked, because I knew as happy and twinkling as everything looked, it was feeling pretty heavy, too.

"We're okay," she said, and I smiled at the automatic we. "I mean, it's hard. Three days until Christmas and every day it feels like something else reaches out and chokes me. Hmm. Maybe more like every other hour. It's all complicated. I mean, from wondering whether I should send out Christmas cards – I didn't by the way, and I think that deserves some sort of prize – to deciding which decorations to give away to which kids. And do I keep some for David? Do I keep some for Summer? And do I have to keep some things for Josie, and what about the grandbabies who aren't born yet? They won't even know Randall. They are not going to care about his Tennessee Vols mini stockings. And that feels wrong."

She paused, her hand going to the table between our rocking chairs. There was no wine there yet, Jessie girl. We giggled at the same time.

"It's so weird," she continued, shaking her head. "I mean, I'm not complaining—"

I held up my hand at that. I wasn't always great at listening. "Girl, you don't have to qualify it to me. I understand what you mean. It's not the same. It's just not the same."

I felt like Jessie always wanted to make sure I felt okay because my *first husband* (still getting used to that phrase, even though I rarely thought of Tony so it only came up a few times, in my head) had been gone a lot longer than hers. It wasn't even close to the same. Tony was, pardon me but, a selfish, cowardly asshole who left us but was still alive and well and up until the recent clandestine message, had forgotten we existed. The only tiny, removed form of communication from him was the garnishing of his wages that had ended, nine years ago on Moni's 18th birthday. She hadn't even graduated high school yet and I could have fought him, but I digress. Randall loved Jessie until the very end. He adored their kids. He did everything in the world he could for them, took Sam as his own without a single hesitation.

So the loss of Randall was beyond different. There's no comparing grief anyway. I wish people would stop that. How they grieve, what they grieve, the timing of grief, which lasts forever, really, should not be compared. It's all personal, which also means none of it is anyone's business.

"Sooo how is Paul doing?" I asked, because hopefully that was a simpler answer for her.

"You know Paul." She smiled the secret smile that I knew was her Paul Smile. "He's doing really well. He has his moments, too, but certainly not, you know, every other hour. He's getting together with Danielle and Katy tomorrow afternoon. I know he's sad about Julie not coming, but he's kinda relieved too. God only knows what that entails since David's not coming either." I involuntarily grimaced. *That boy.* "I thought she might change her mind at the last minute," Jessie sighed. "I don't want to deal with her BS either, but I don't want Paul to be any sadder or lonelier than he might be anyway."

"Paul hasn't been lonely since you moved into this house," I said, and as if on cue, the romantic equivalent of her magical unicorn walked outside with a tray. *A tray!*

I waited with forced patience while he set the magical array of mimosas, biscuits, cheese, and jam on the table and wrapped him up with as much fervor as I'd given Jess. I think he was almost my favorite non-Sheldon-Moni-or-Nora person in the world.

He laughed when I didn't let go. "Mags! Welcome home!"

"You are already the best host ever," I said, finally stepping back to look at him. He was still too thin, and his stubble was looking a little wild, but his green eyes were as warm and twinkly as ever. Clearly my girl was good for his soul. "Thank you and I'm sorry for crashing your peaceful, blissful beach cottage…"

More laughter. "You know Katy gets here in the morning, right? There will not be peace within 30 miles of this place. And Nora is inside *dusting the freaking bookshelves.*"

Jessie stood right up at that to, I was sure, go scold her niece. My oldest daughter was an over-compensator if there ever was one. Dusting, for crying out loud. Paul and I glanced at each other and laughed some more. It felt good to be on their porch.

...

After our front-porch brunch, we went shopping for Christmas dinner(s) – there's always more than one – with Nora and Moni. Then we went to Mikayla's and loved the baby for an hour. We left the cousins there so Jess and I could do some last-minute gift-shopping. We all had dinner at Sam and Abby's house, BBQ from Hog Heaven with all the fixin's. I was stuffed and happy when we returned to Jessie's house. Paul was taking a "quick run" *(whaaaaaat?)* and after I finally unpacked in my amazing little guest suite, Jessie ushered me upstairs for her signature nightcap (tea, honey, and whiskey), closing the door of the master bedroom behind us.

I took in every detail. It was definitely a departure from the room she'd shared with Randall and tried to tweak for a life with Paul, God bless them. The bright, boho colors and patterns had been replaced by a more subdued, layered palette… sage, which by sound and smell was practically synonymous with Paul, robin's egg blue, and because Jessie needed some loudness in her surroundings, garnet red. Her beachy white furniture had been replaced with gray-washed pine, a soft white rug covering the bamboo floor. The only contrasting color in the room was navy, on the room-darkening Roman shades that were rolled up above the balcony doors.

"This is perfect," I said, settling with my mug on one of the chairs flanking those windows. "I can't believe you have one of those fake fireplaces in here. Has he ever experienced one of your hot flashes?"

"It's not fake; it's portable!" she laughed. "And he pretends not to notice. But I made him promise he won't use this unless it's below 40 degrees or I am out of the state."

"As if you'd go that far from him," I said.

"You're just as smitten as I am, and you're here without Shel-don," she protested. I was literally the only person alive who called my husband by his full name. I loved its intrinsic awkwardness. What kind of black man was named Sheldon? The kind who had raised two children largely on his own, who was a lawyer and in a bike gang (made up of lawyers), and whom everyone but his second wife called Don.

"And I miss him like crazy," I said. "Does Paul run... a lot?"

"Ever since he got clearance," she said, shaking her head in the same disbelief I felt. "Apparently his bionic ankle is stronger than the other one, and as long as he doesn't overdo it and keeps up some strengthening, it's all good."

"What a damn year," I sighed. Paul had some sort of ligament reconstruction during his breakup with Jessie, and suddenly he was in training for a 10K or something. There really was a surprise of some sort around every little corner.

We talked back and forth about new life with new men, sipping our spiked drinks and interjecting with this and that about our kids. It felt like I'd never moved away, with just one nagging thought pressing into the back of my mind. I waited until she made the tiniest mention of David. That was my open door.

"So, is David still keeping in touch with, um, your

brother?" I asked, trying so hard to be caszh, cas, cajj, casual. Jessie scrunched up her whole face. "You mean your ex-husband?"

"He was your brother first."

"Touché. But he's your baby daddy for-eva..."

"He's your brother forever, too," I said. "And you still haven't answered the question."

She shrugged. "I think so. They're Facebook friends, anyway. Don't ask me how I know."

"We have the same talent," I said. "Have you looked up Sheldon's ex yet?" I already knew the answer.

"Candy," she said, shaking her head. "Sheldon and Candy. It was never meant to last."

"He was just Don to her," I said. "She did not know he was Sheldon in his *soul*."

We laughed some more. "Anyway, why ask about Tony? I thought about sending him a message to leave David alone, or at least to tread carefully, back when David was still in Arizona, but it seems moot now. Why are you asking me?"

Why was I? Why hadn't I just answered Tony myself? Why was I a little afraid to tell her I'd heard from him? There was no question of Jessie's loyalty, not between Tony and me. She might have grown up with him, but she was growing old with me.

"I'm just... curious..." I finally said. I wasn't ready. Tony had torn me inside-out 20 years ago. There was literally never an explanation for him leaving, no major signs leading up to it, no closure, and certainly no apology. But there was hard-won peace, and he'd been out of my system for 10 million years. Why was I feeling something now, now when I was finally married again?

She narrowed her eyes. I knew she didn't believe me. But we were both buzzed and tired from a day of activities and *dranks*, and neither of us was ready to chase it down. We'd have plenty of time at the spa the next day.

"You wanna scroll Julie's page?" I asked.

We both laughed again. It felt good to laugh with her. I was a little surprised and mostly proud when she shook her head. It was best to leave the past in the past and leave alone people who didn't want us. Fa-la-la-la-la.

[6]

"Daddy, I really can't believe this is how I'm spending a kid-free evening."

Danielle was huffing and puffing next to Paul. He refused to feel bad until he saw how red her face was and that, possibly, the sweat on her shirt might be a milk leak. That hadn't happened in months; Vivi was 10-months-old already. Already.

He and Jess talked about that part a lot, how Leah and Randall would have so many grandkids they would never hold, never know. It gave him peace that Leah had spent so much time with Christian, Danielle's first. They did art together and baked and read together. Leah loved having a little boy around. She said it made her feel like she could redeem Paul's boyhood a little, to lavish Christian with love and attention and quality experiences. He hoped Christian would remember her. Paul was going to try his best to ensure that he would.

Vivi had been held and dressed up by Leah for 35 days before Leah was killed. It was not enough, never would be.

"Seriously, Daddy. Enough. Julie is the runner, not us. And not you, for that matter." Katy was not in any way red-faced, but she had complained during the entire two rather-sluggish miles they'd taken around Market Common.

"You were a pretty enthusiastic runner when he bought you those shoes," Danielle observed. They'd stopped at the local running store so Paul could quickly grab a new handheld water bottle, maybe some socks. They'd ended up being there for almost an hour while Katy got her "gait assessment" and spent some time assessing the young-ish male owner who was not wearing a wedding ring, as she had pointed out seventeen times.

"They do feel really good," Katy said, totally nonplussed by her big sister. "Maybe I could run. 'specially if Nick was coaching me."

Nick. She couldn't remember to pick up the wine Jessie liked on her way from Wilmington, or to bring the copy of *The Christmas Story* she'd taken from the house before he sold it, but she was now on first-name basis with the running store owner.

Oh Katy. Three minutes into their excursion, she'd actually uttered, "Mama would *die* if she saw you running!" Paul burst out laughing, but Danielle hit her sister's shoulder with leftover-teenage ferocity. Katy yelped and apologized. Danielle scolded Paul for laughing. And then they worked their way through the next 20 minutes while Paul thought of all the ways Leah would, in fact, be surprised at how he was living these days.

"You always hated it," Danielle said now, trying to discreetly change her shirt on the other side of the Jeep. "I know you did it sometimes for Mama's sake, just like Katy and I did, but... you really hated it."

"Mostly because it hated me," Paul answered, mopping the sweat of his forehead. "I get it now, though. It clears my head. It balances out all the sweet tea and donuts. It's a win-win."

"As long as you don't blow out your other ankle," Katy quipped.

"Good God, you're on a roll today," Danielle snapped.

"It's fine," Paul said, shaking his head. He never expected Katy to be gentle or even considerate, though he would have welcomed a little show of either that day. "I mean, my other ankle is fine. All my parts are fine. Katy, I know you probably already used every ounce of niceness you have to give this year, but if you can scrape up a little to help us get through Christmas, that would be excellent."

"Yes, sir," Katy muttered.

"Are you sure we shouldn't go home and shower before we have dinner?" Danielle asked.

"If you go home now, Christian and Vivi won't let you leave again," he answered. "It's okay. It's nice out. We can eat outside if that makes you feel more comfortable."

After methodically swiping at herself with aqua wipes, Danielle balled them up, threw them in the front seat trash bag, and crossed over to the driver side door, where she promptly hugged him and cried. And cried.

Paul took a moment to glance at Katy, who was looking as much *away* as she could. She could only express grief on her own timeline, and this clearly wasn't it. Danielle was shaking from the power of her sobs, and Paul felt his own insides waver. She'd taken on so much that year, handling whatever her shock-ridden father could not in the days right after the accident, responding in positivity and grace and acceptance when he and Jessie shared their relationship status, even taking his dumb ass in when he'd moved out of Jessie's with no place to go. Had he even seen her cry, really cry, since Leah died? He wasn't sure he had.

"I love you so much, baby," he said softly, stroking her hair. "Mama would be so proud of you."

They were clichés, and normally Paul hated those, but there were no more perfect words, or more true ones. In a year that had changed everything he knew, those two bits of truth were just about all he had left to give his eldest daughter.

...

"God bleeeeeeeesssss..." Katy proclaimed. "Why have I never been here?"

Paul briefly looked up from his Fiesta Crepé, add bacon, to Katy's beaming face, inhaling her Nutella-smothered Belgian waffle. Jessie had taught Paul a few life-changing methods since they'd begun their new relationship, and one of them was the healing, unifying, comforting, magical power of good, and sometimes fancy, food.

And so instead of heading up the road to Burky's for burgers and shakes and the best fries ever, Paul asked Danielle to pick where they'd eat, and she'd chosen Crepé Creations, the name of which would have made him roll his eyes and simply say "No," a few months ago; that is, a few months and a lifetime ago, the *before*.

Danielle swallowed her mouthful of Cordon Bleu Chicken – Paul had to keep himself from snatching a bite – and gave Katy a generous smile. (Food = Magic). "You want to know the truth? Mama took me here once, when I was pregnant with Vivi, and ever since, I have only come back by myself. Granted, that's been twice, maybe? I'm never alone. But I wanted to keep it our little place. Until today. It feels right today."

Paul and Katy nodded with the appropriate solemnity, and then Katy regrouped. "I know this is probably an unpopular opinion, but I wish Julie was here."

Danielle took another bite, shifting uncomfortably in her seat. Paul drained his tea, unsure if there was any correct response or any need for one.

"Can we call her?" Katy pressed.

Danielle looked at him, questioningly.

Paul shrugged. "Can it wait until we finish our dinner?" Danielle nodded and Katy put her phone down, also shrugging. He'd at least learned, in almost 30 years of parenting three daughters, the precarious balance of their three personalities, and his own.

Once the plates were cleared and dessert was ordered, Katy and Danielle each fluffed their hair (well, *foofed*, they called it. He wasn't sure that was a real word), and Katy dialed.

Paul always thought it was at most, rude, and at least, weird, to Facetime from public places. He was grateful they were sitting outside, where it wasn't overly crowded on the 60-degree evening. More sensible people were eating inside, although, he noted, this weather was still a little on the warm side for Jessie.

Julie picked up during the very first ring. He'd only talked to her a handful of times since he and Jessie *really* moved in together; that was how he had to differentiate, because the first time felt colossally rushed, foolish, humiliating, and painful when he thought about it now. He'd been the one to rationalize all of it, and he'd been just as not-ready for it as Jessie had been.

But now? Now was perfect timing, as far as he was concerned. Julie didn't say much. He supposed she was acquiesced to the fact that her 60-something-year-old father was capable of some logical decisions, and she also bore her share of humiliation from her ill-fated relationship with her soon-to-be-stepbrother.

Dear Jesus. Their lives were weird.

Mostly, Julie struggled with not feeling needed. She couldn't leave her new job in Arizona to help him recover from his surgery, which was probably the most Paul had actually needed anyone in his adult life. And now that he was physically whole and healthily in love, the latter which she resented, she had no idea what her place was.

"Merry almost-Christmas, Jules!" he called out with as much exuberance as he could muster. He couldn't help feeling a little nervous. She was so much like Leah, noticing everything, trying to be polite but always a little cynical, even critical at times. She loved whom she loved, but often from afar. She didn't like messy. Paul's beard was messy, and so was his mood.

"Hi Daddy," she said, much more calmly, as reserved as he'd expected. She didn't even greet her sisters, whom he assumed she communicated with daily. She only had eyes for him, and it made him even more anxious.

"How you doing, kiddo?" He let his voice soften, trying so hard to be natural. She was hard, rock hard, on the outside, but he knew she was no less heartbroken than Danielle and no less impassioned than Katy.

Julie's response was filled with work and church stories, all carefully crafted and largely emotionless. She asked about Christian and Vivi, about Danielle's husband Matt, about the weather. She did not mention Chad, the man she'd broken up with David for, nor did she mention Jessie, the new house, or when she might come for a visit. She did express excited approval over their pre-dinner run. She even clapped her hands.

"So what are you doing when dinner's over?"

Paul hesitated. "We're going back to Dani's to read *Song of the Stars* with the kids." Might as well just rip off the band-aid.

"Oh," Julie said. "But it's not Christmas Eve yet..." Leah

had read that one on Christmas Eve since Christian had been born.

"We're going to do something a little different this year," Danielle said, simply, evenly, a little steely, as though she was daring Julie to protest, Paul observed.

"I see," Julie said. She didn't ask what, or where, or with whom. Paul would have told her *The Legend of the Candy Cane*, at his home, with Jessie's grandkids, because Danielle and Matt would be with his parents, and that was perfectly okay. They didn't have to try to keep everything the same, because it wasn't. And it never would be.

§[7]

On the other side of town, down on the Marshwalk, Jessie sat at a less-sizeable table than usual with Sam and Abby, Travis (because he was a grandkid but at 17, almost grown), Brittany, Mikayla, and her husband, Altan, who held a sleeping Josie in his arms. They were at Dead Dog Saloon, sitting at a table near Cash's picture on one of the many doggie-memorial walls, with baskets of mostly-untouched hush puppies and wet rings around full soda glasses scattered among them.

On the night before Christmas Eve, the Oakleys were not merry, and for the first time in her tenure as a mother, Jessie was not trying to fix it.

"It's good to have Nora and Moni here," Mikayla offered softly. "I feel like we haven't seen them in forever."

"The wedding was just a few months ago," Brittney responded. Mikayla almost looked confused, but Maggie's wedding had, in fact, been only a little over two months prior to that night. Jessie understood the blurriness on her daughter's face. The timeline of that whole year had run together. Mikayla's first pregnancy had ended almost a year ago, right after what would turn out to be their last Christmas with Randall. That alone would have made any brain a little fuzzy, but adding everything else...

Jessie kind of wanted to put her arms and head down right there on the table and sleep until the new year.

Sam was next to her, his arm protectively around the back of her chair. He was sipping a beer and oddly, seemed to be relaxed for once. He had taken the following week off work, and the day after Christmas, he and Abby and the kids were going to Disney World. Jess was happy for them. She kind of wished she were going, too.

How many different things do you want, Jess? Disney isn't restful. A family Christmas isn't quiet. And Paul isn't Randall.

Stop. It. She wasn't sure if that voice in her head was Maggie's or Paul's. Oddly enough, or not, she checked her phone and saw a text from Morgan, her pastor's wife and local bestie these days. And all it said was, "I know you're with your kids tonight, so you don't have to respond. Just reminding you that it's okay to enjoy the moment, welcome the sadness, *and* it's okay to be thankful for Paul," followed by the prayer and red heart emojis, alternating across three lines.

I'm thankful for YOU! she texted back, and then put her phone away.

"What should I bring tomorrow night, Mama?" Brittney asked, dipping a hush puppy into honey butter. Finally. What an ice breaker.

Jessie shrugged, feeling strangely ambivalent toward the food. "Ask Aunt Maggie. She's in charge of the menu."

Brittney fake-coughed while everyone else giggled. Everyone else, save for Travis, already knew, because they'd been directed to Maggie one-by-one. Brittney never asked until the last minute, which is why she usually brought drinks.

"You better get to the store before the artisan soda and eggnog is all gone, sissy," Sam teased. Jessie felt her cheeks get pleasantly warm at the word *sissy*. One thing she was uncomplicatedly grateful for was that her children had much closer relationships with each other than she'd ever had with Tony.

Even if – "I still can't believe David isn't coming." Travis had actually set *his* phone down and broken his informal vow of silence. "It's bad enough…"

And that was all he said. It was enough. David and Travis were only three years apart and much more like brothers than uncle-nephew.

Sam raised one eyebrow across the table at his oldest son, and Abby handed Travis a hush puppy. He popped it in, softened a little, but stayed in his feelings.

Yep, Jessie thought. *That time was definitely Maggie. "In your feelings" is a Maggie thing. And Travis is there, disappointed and downright mad. Like the rest of us.*

"Do you think he's really staying away because of some bathroom project?" Altan asked. Usually, Jessie's adored son-in-law was better at reading the room. *Of course* no one believed that.

"*Of course* no one believes that," Brittney answered. "He's staying away because he's not ready to face the music and admit he was wrong for moving away with Julie."

"He already admitted that," Sam said.

"But he said he was going to come for a whole *month* before his classes started," Travis said.

Mikayla nodded. "He did say that. And he hasn't even met Josie."

The table erupted then, a few of them counting off the

ways David could handle himself differently, the balance of them taking up for him, as he was the baby after all (Sam's own words).

"Stop it," Jessie said loudly, right after the server stepped away. She sounded much more like Randall than she sounded like herself.

"No one wishes David was coming home more than I do," she said, only a touch more softly. "Well, Trav, except for maybe you." They smiled at each other. "But just like we all have our reasons for being here, he has his reasons for staying away. And for this Christmas, and maybe all the rest of them, we have to give each other permission to face the joy and pain—" *...are like sunshine and rain. Oh, give it to me, Rob Bass...* definitely her own voice... "—exactly how we need to face it. Alone. Together. Here. Away. Maybe a combination of all of it. Like, for those of you who don't know, the biggest reason Maggie is 'hosting' Christmas Eve tomorrow night is because she and Paul insisted I spend some time alone tomorrow. So instead of compiling lasagna and hand-breading fish, I'll be at the beach. Alone. Sad. Missing your Dad."

"But... you have Paul..."

Jessie had probably not snapped at Mikayla, her most emotional child, since either Kayla's puberty or the onset of Jessie's menopause, but here they were. "How many times do I have to say this? Being with Paul doesn't mean I don't miss your dad, *my husband.* He was *my husband!* Am I not allowed to mourn? Everyone else can take trips and have babies and make plans and still miss him, but not me? It's all or nothing for me?!"

Well. That got a little louder than she'd meant. "Excuse me," she muttered, dropping her napkin in her chair and finding her way to the bathroom.

She so badly wanted to text Paul. But she also so badly

hoped he was having his own, less awkward time with his own kids.. She hoped he felt free, that Danielle and Katy were seeing him as a person and not just their dad, that they were remembering happy moments with Leah and not only being sad.

It really seemed like too much to ask, all of it. She started to text Maggie, and decided better of that, too. Sheldon and the rest of their clan were on their way from Greenville, and she was sure Maggie was already at their rental, decorating with the masses of extra holiday stuff she and Jessie had retrieved from storage. *You're a grownup,* she pep-talked herself. *You're not on a game show. You don't need to phone a friend.* And then she typed into her phone:

I hope y'all are resting before your festivities start. Can't wait to see you at church tomorrow. Everything is fine and I don't want to bother you... I just... I don't know if I'm doing 'this' right, and there probably isn't a 'right.' Just say a prayer for the kids and me. I know you already do. I love y'all. So much.

She hit send. She looked in the mirror and sighed. In spite of supposedly-illuminating eye makeup, a dang decent tan for December, and the fact that she was 20 whole pounds lighter than she was at the Fourth of July, she looked tired, and she felt old.

"You can do this." At that moment, her phone vibrated. Morgan, probably deep into kitchen projects, had "loved" her message. Her husband Carter, Jessie's pastor, one of Randall's closest friends, and frankly, one of Jessie's, sent his own response:

Jess, we love you, too. All of you. You're RIGHT... there is no 'right.' Just follow what God is putting on your heart. Maybe in this hard and holy season, it is simply to listen and receive... and as you wish for us, to rest. You have worked hard this year, healing and helping and rebuilding. Maybe take 'silent night' as an invitation. *Don't fix anything. Just behold the wonders of His love.*

Through the tears streaming down Jessie's face, she saw Morgan's follow-up message and laughed out loud:

That was really Jesus-y. But he's right.

Baking two Dutch apple pies. Dropping one to you tomorrow. XXOO

Doing it right? Doing it wrong? Whatever she had done in her life, she was surrounded by the most amazing, loving, steadfast, on-time people in the world. She was more full of gratitude than her house was about to be full of excessive cheese and cookies. She had to keep telling herself it was okay to be thankful *and* heartbroken.

As she opened the door to the bathroom, Abby was stepping inside.

"You're the lucky one they sent? Again?"

Abby laughed as Jessie threw her arms around her. "They know you're never mad at me..." she said, and it was true. "But your and Travis' blue crab nachos just arrived, and they're either going to get soggy or eaten by that skinny teenager if you don't come back."

Walking with an arm around her, Jessie said, "I never left."

...

Forty-five minutes later, the table was a hot mess and they were all either rubbing their own bellies or ordering desserts. Jessie could not stomach another bite, but warmth had settled over her. There was nothing like sharing junk-food disguised as decadence with her grandson, and having a few somber and festive toasts with her adult children, to remind her that even though life was complicated, loving her family was anything but.

The perfunctory Facetime to David was only a little awkward. He was near the lit firepit in the backyard of

Randall's sister Christy and her husband Joel. Jessie could almost smell the mountain air, and she decided right then that she would plan a trip there, just her, as soon as the holidays were over. She wasn't going to be one of those mothers who insisted the kids come to her. She was still young and had means and ability. She was going to travel. She was going to stay in David's life and remind him that no matter what mistakes he might make, he would always have her love and encouragement.

Travis still seemed glum when they started saying goodnight, and Mikayla still seemed a bit fragile at being admonished, but Jessie kept reviewing Carter's words in her head. This season was hard, so hard, but it was holy. Thank God they had a Randall to miss. Thank God they had each other to keep his memory alive. Thank God they had so much ahead of them, some of their best days still to come.

Jessie held on to that thought, fighting hard to flee, as she returned home to a quiet and dark house. With Maggie's crew down the street, Katy had taken up residence in the guest suite. She smiled as she got some water and heard Reese Witherspoon's voice blaring from the TV and smelled cinnamon spice candles from the other side of the pocket door. Katy brought life and energy to wherever she was, and Jessie was grateful that her energy was usually positive.

She let the fatigue of the last few days settle in as she climbed the stairs. She'd eaten too much cheese and drank too much alcohol the past few days. Her sacred morning at the beach was going to include water with lemon and some peace and quiet.

Paul was unmaking the bed when she walked in. She dropped her purse on the ground by the nightstand, set her water atop it, and flung herself over the covers.

"Are you okay?" he asked, and then they both giggled because it was such a stupid question, confusing and pointless and without a real answer.

She yawned before she answered. "It's fine," she said, and laughed a little more. "It's just heavy, and I'm sad. I'm sad for you, and I'm sad for me. I'm sad that I don't really know how to help anyone, and mostly I'm just really sad for our kids. And I think I'm a little bit drunk, too."

Her sweet Paul, a quietly recovered alcoholic, sober for over 20 years, deadpanned, "You and Maggie have been drinking for 48 straight hours."

Damnit. She could not argue. *Water. Just water tomorrow.*

She didn't think he was mad about it. He usually didn't say a word, and drinking *usually* didn't seem to bother him. There were too many feelings *all up in there* that night for her to tell what was what. But without another word, he got under the covers, and she retreated to the bathroom to do all her things, shower, lotion, floss, ponder a boob lift, pray, retreat to the bedroom. She'd skip her whiskey-laced tea that night. She really had had enough.

They both had, she supposed.

As she slipped beneath the covers, he gave her another small smile and closed his eyes. He was already drifting. She couldn't help wondering for the eight-millionth time, as she watched him with so much fondness that it made her heart race, for the eight-millionth time, how this whole thing went for other people. How did people *simply* grieve for a husband, for their babies' daddy, for the life they thought they were going to have? She knew it wasn't any easier. But was it less complicated? Was it somehow more navigable when it was *just* that one kind of heartbreak, and not layered on top of watching the same impossible, relentless anguish in someone else you loved so fiercely?

She knew there was no answer to that, that it was one of *eight-million* questions for which she would never have an answer. So she tried not to let her eyes linger on his dozing form while she drew herself a little closer to him. They kept the house cold at night, a nod to her post-menopausal internal thermostat and in memoriam of the years she slept with a balcony door open to let in the ocean breeze. She missed it some, even though she'd sold her own house during her break-up with Paul, not thinking for a moment they would ever live together again. She wouldn't trade their new home, not for anything except, well, the freedom of simpler answers and less complicated questions.

"I can hear you," Paul murmured, turning over with one eye peering at her. "When you think that hard, it's audible. Or you actually have some sort of telepathy."

"Wouldn't that mean *you* have telepathy? Which, by the way, I am certain you do. You're the one who *heard* me looking at you…"

"And wondering if I was okay. And trying not to think about you not being okay. And trying to keep yourself from…"

He didn't finish. And she was so relieved. He could have said *eight million* different things to her and at least seven million, nine hundred thousand, nine-hundred, ninety-four would have made her feel better. But—

His arms wrapped around her, cradled her, and he pulled her against him so that every part of her was being enveloped or touched by a part of him. There were no more words. He was as raw and worn as she was. She felt the moisture on his cheeks mingle with hers. She heard the long inhale as he steadied himself against her. His hands ran over her head and stroked her hair, even as hers caressed his neck, wiped one of the tears that had traveled there.

"We're almost there," he whispered.

"It's just the first one. The first Christmas. And then there are more birthdays, and births, and the anniversary.

One year. It hasn't even been a year. And there is a lifetime ahead. Their lives. Their weddings and babies and when we… go…"

She stopped when she felt him shaking, worried and surprised and then—

"Oh, Paul…"

He lifted his head from the pillow and confirmed that his face was red, from laughter.

"Don't kill us off yet, Jess!" His laugher actually turned into a whoop. There were fresh tears popping into his eyes, illuminated by the light of the TV and the teeny Christmas tree sitting on their dresser. He was laughing. *Laughing.*

"Paul!" But it was hard to admonish him when she was cracking up herself.

The laughter didn't stop. He laughed after she stopped. He laughed while she scooted closer to him. He laughed while she kissed his neck, right in the spot that usually calmed him down (although she was enjoying the excitement). He laughed when her tongue darted around his ear and her hands clasped his hips, scrunching down his shorts and then pulling him closer.

He swiftly and a little roughly turned her onto her back, deftly removed her tank top, and lay himself on top of her. He wasn't laughing anymore.

...

Jessie wished she could sleep like Paul. After they'd made love, he'd returned from the bathroom all freshened up and was passed out in approximately 36 seconds. She had taken another quick shower, read two chapters of Elin Hilderbrand back in the Bahamas, and texted a little with Mikayla until she seemed set back at ease. As she was plugging in her phone, another message popped up.

Maggie: *You up?*

Jessie: *Of course. It's barely midnight.*

Maggie: *Listen sister, I need to tell you something. It's bugging me. Can you come outside?*

Was she flippin' kidding? *Outside?* Was the hellmouth opening or were she and Sheldon having a fight?

Hang on.

She didn't bother with shoes or anything else. Surely Katy was tucked in for the night and the only people who might be on the streets in Surfside were crazy runners or sneaky teenagers, and neither kind would notice her.

"What the hell, sister?" Ooch. It was actually a little cool outside. Jessie silently thanked the heavens. Maggie was standing there wrapped in a shawl and possibly a bedspread. She looked ridiculous and still radiant. Jessie looked beyond her to the street and saw Sheldon sitting there in his running Lexus RX. He waved sheepishly.

"Why did you make that man drive you here at this hour? Are you nuts?"

"I know. I'm sorry. But something happened and I should have told you!"

"Maggie. You could have *called*. What in the world?"

Maggie was rarely if ever anxious. Jessie often busted her chops since she was anxious at least half the time. But she was pulling at the loose threads on the tattered coverlet and not looking Jessie in the eye.

"Who else is coming to Christmas, Mags?" Surely it couldn't be any more serious than that.

Maggie looked confused, then amused, then beleaguered all over again.

"Have you heard from Tony?" she finally asked.

"Tony?" Jessie shook her head. She really needed to sleep. No idea what Maggie was talking abou—

"*Tony?!*"

"Dear Jesus, Joey Tribbiani. Get there faster!" Maggie exclaimed.

"Why are you asking me about him again? I hear from him so little that his *name* doesn't register, Maggie. What is happening here?"

"You haven't answered, though."

"Maggie!"

Maggie raised one eyebrow and tapped her foot. Jessie looked straight in the driver's window and gave Sheldon the most Italian gesture she could summon in her state of confusion and exhaustion: she threw her hands in the air in such a way that he must understand her unspoken words, "Your wife is batshit crazy. Please come retrieve her from my driveway."

He shrugged, looking confused himself. She turned back to Maggie and heard the rage simmering in her voice. "No. I have not heard from Tony. Not in months, since right after Randall, and not years before that. Who. Cares?"

"He keeps messaging me," Maggie said, and all her bravado deflated from her. She was now a week-old party balloon, forlornly stuck to the top of a wall by a just-sticky-enough piece of tape.

"What?"

"He sent me a Facebook message, right before we came here, and I blocked him. Then he sent me an Instagram message. I blocked him. And tonight, he sent me one on Linked In, so I finally answered and told him Merry Christmas, please stop with the tomfuckery."

"Fa-la-la-la-la," she whispered. *Friggen Tony.*

"What did he want?"

Maggie adjusted her blankies and looked anxiously back at Sheldon, who was doing his best to pretend not to see any of it. Jessie swatted her shoulder. "Woman. What?!"

"We should sit."

"I don't believe this. I am not making that man wait in the street while you engage in drama. Spit it out, Margarete

Diana Dunn. Now."

"Well. He told me why he's stayed away all these years. I mean, the message was kinda brief and I didn't answer him yet, but I felt like you should know. And…" she tugged another time at the thread. Gosh, it was an ugly bedspread. "I need you to help me know how to respond."

Jessie rolled her eyes, even though there was no one to see the gesture in the darkness. "Sister, I appreciate it, but do you seriously not remember all of a sudden that I could not care less? Tony has been absent from my life longer than he's been absent from yours. He wasn't invested in the births of my children, or the death of my child, or the death of my husband. I don't know what he does and I don't even have the capacity to care. Okay? Take Sheldon. Go to your beach house. Enjoy your first magical Christmas together! The hell with my brother!" *And peace on earth, good will to men,* chimed the still small voice in her head.

Maggie looked unconvinced and acquiesced all at once. She nodded and hugged Jessie, then turned to her husband's car.

Jessie stood there watching her, trying not to let rage overtake her. She needed to sleep. Of all the damned things to come in and join the overcrowded complexities of this holiday, the last she would have expected was her brother, supposedly trying to make some sort of amends, after all these mostly-silent years.

After Sheldon and Maggie were out of sight, she crept back through the front door and leaned against it, staring into the expanse of their living room. It took her breath away how much she loved it… the hodge-podge of furniture, the books everywhere, the wood-paneled ceiling, the sparkles of emerald green, turquoise, hints of red, and white, finally some white, on the gray-washed background of everything. She never dreamed she would love another home as much as the one she and Randall had made for 10 years on the second row from the beach, but this one immediately felt warm and light and enveloping. She and Paul had bought a huge, real Christmas tree directly from the Scouts and dazzled it with 800 twinkling lights and every ornament they felt like hanging, no themes or color schemes. The tree skirt was hand-knit by Jessie's grandmother, originally a blanket with all the perfect holiday colors. She loved it. She wanted to feel perfectly peaceful there, and in spite of all the obstacles grief and blending brought, she was close. She was not going to let Tony ruin it.

Resisting the urge to give up and brew coffee, she got back upstairs and slid back next to Paul, who clearly hadn't been stirred by More Adventures with Jessie and Maggie. But her phone was lit with another message. Seriously? It was going on one in the morning and didn't any of her people sleep?

The contact read "David." And the content read,

"Mama. I'm gonna come. See you in time for dinner tomorrow." Sunglasses emoji, blue heart emoji.

It was the missing *peace*, she thought. Smiling, she set the phone on the bedside face down and drifted to sleep at Paul's side.

[8]

"That smells goooooood." Sheldon's strong arms wrapped around my waist and nearly sent my mixing spoon flying into the air. I should have been mad but instead I was laughin'. The last 24 hours had carried more heaviness than I'd intended to let in, but here in Jessie's kitchen, mixing my sweet potato soufflé, listening to Nat and Johnny and Bing, and being squeezed by that beautiful man, it was hard to be anything but happy. I mean, joy to the bless-ed world.

"You can't have any," I told him, offering him a kiss in lieu of a brown-sugar-maple-syrup-laden spoonful. "Go play!"

I giggled as he nuzzled my neck. We swayed a bit to "Here Comes Santa Claus," because Mr. Mathis can make even silly carols a little bit sexy, and then we heard a throat clear. I turned around to see Nora and Paul, standing in the doorway adjacent to the Cousin Nook, smirking at us.

"Need some help, Mama?" Nora asked. I would have

53

elbowed her if I hadn't had to cross the room to do it.

"As a matter of fact, I do. Beer bread is mixed but it needs to go in the oven, and I have the final Food Lions list right here." Cross me, why don't you, child? I can flirt and get dinner together at the same dang time.

None of us had had a traditional Thanksgiving dinner for Thanksgiving, so we were having it that night. The smoked turkey was coming from the butcher shop, 'cause ain't nobody got time for that, but the rest was coming from my own two hands, with a little help from my daughters and nieces, because Jessie would love it, and she deserved it.

"You ready to go?" Paul asked, facing my husband. They were dressed for a run. Weirdos.

"Let's do it!" Sheldon said with much exuberance, which I would have made fun of except he kissed me one more time with equal enthusiasm, audience or not.

Nora watched me watch them walk out the door. "Don't say a word," I said, turning back to my mixing bowl, but she just smiled.

"Mama, shush. He's so good for you! Now what could you possibly need from the store *again*? There is enough here to feed—"

She cut herself off and put the bread for my dressing in the oven. Whatever the end of that sentence was, army, circus, village, we had it. And extra because God knew who else was going to show up. Travis' girlfriend Cali was the latest added to the list, followed by the very welcome announcement from Jessie that her prodigal baby boy would be coming home just in time for the crudités.

"You taking anyone with you?" I asked. Our newly-blended bunch was still understandably formal with each other. I doubted there was a sibling-group-text or anything like that, so I was equally thankful for the lack of drama and hopeful for a little bonding.

"Actually, everyone else was meeting Abby and the kids at the park for awhile. It's so nice out. I forget about this beach weather. Never thought I'd miss it."

She looked casual as she collected Jessie's shopping bags from the hook by the door. "You need *anything* else besides this stuff, Mama? Because I will not be returning to that madhouse after I get your," she glanced down at the list, "cinnamon sticks, *fresh* tortilla chips, and *cupcakes*?! Really, Mama?!"

"Don't you dare question me," I laughed. "I need a gluten-free dipping option. And have you watched *A Very Brady Christmas*, lately? Eddie and Sheldon *ate* those brownies I had set aside for tonight. We can't not have kid-friendly desserts. And they are not getting the salted caramel cheesecake. Some forms of indulgence simply can't be appreciated by anyone under 25."

"Summer will be mad," Nora said with a grin.

"Summer will get over it. Be right back? I'll make us some mimosas."

Nora kissed me and said too-softly, "I'm not drinking."

"Wait, what?"

I put my hand on my eldest's smooth cheek and attempted to stare into her soul.

"I stopped drinking right after your wedding."

"Why?"

Twenty-six immediate hypotheses formulated in my brain, but one specific one was at the forefront.

"I drank too much that night."

"Okay. Didn't we all?..." It had been a pretty fantastic night, except for Jessie being in double mourning (she and Paul were still broken up then). Actually, I'd never tell her, but her sadness was probably the reason for my third and fourth lemon drops. It only took two, but there they were...

"I drank too much and acted out, Mama." Why did this

30-year-old suddenly look 16? Was she pregnant or was it something else? And why was I suddenly thinking of Tony again? *Why* had he wormed his way back into my head when I should have finally been rid of him once and for all?

"Okay, darlin', help a sister out here. What do you mean, exactly? What did you do?"

I grabbed both of her hands, ensuring she couldn't walk away and would face extreme awkwardness trying to look away. Her voice *sounded* like my 16-year-old Nora, the one who "experimented" all through her junior year, with having girlfriends, being agnostic, and smoking pot under the football bleachers when she was supposed to be playing the flute in the marching band. We barely survived that year.

"I'm just gonna list them for you, okay? And then I'm going to go buy cupcakes."

With the exception of her junior year, which I eventually attributed to hormones peaking while Mercury was in retrograde and Justin was ripping Janet's top off during the Super Bowl, Nora was always methodical, organized, and reliable. I attributed that to her father abandoning her when she was nine-years-old and her mother subsequently never, not once, losing her *ish* in front of her daughters. I probably should have. I should have let them see what a struggle it was so they would know it was okay to ask for help, and it was okay to be mad, and we need to process feelings in a healthy way, and—

I nodded at her. And smiled.

"I drank too much at your wedding, but I had been drinking too much for months before that. I was seeing someone, and they, well, she, broke it off with me, and I was lost there for awhile. So at your wedding, once I reached critical mass, I was dancing with, you know, Some Guy, some guy Brittney knew from freaking high school who was there with his dad, who apparently works at your bank? Or goes to your church? I don't know. What kind of a grown man is his dad's plus-one at a wedding? Anyway. We danced. And then we left together. And we slept together. And he asked me to leave afterwards, because he lives with his dad, too. And then I was just mad. Mad at myself for not even knowing myself. Mad that this idiot brought me home knowing I wouldn't be spending the night. Mad that there are 30-year-olds out there who don't have to worry about where to live. *Mama, I know you did everything in the world for me!* I don't resent anything you did or didn't do. But living in Charlotte is expensive sometimes, and it would have been nice... just... *nice*... to have a dad to call and say, 'Hey. Can you float me a little rent this month? Can I move out to Phoenix and chill with you for a minute in between jobs?' That's how it always seems to be for other people. At least, it did that night, when I was out of my mind and jilted, again."

I waited, so many words being bitten on my tongue. I had a feeling what was coming next. She'd veered quite dramatically from her simple list. This was Mount St. Nora, erupting. It had happened approximately three times in her whole life, save for the year of our Lord, 2004.

"So when I got back to our house, I called my Dad. It was only 10pm in Arizona, and we've been talking ever since. So he knows..."

Recite a Bible verse, Maggie. The Lord is my shepherd. For the Lord God is a sun and a shield. Proverbs-freaking-31. Jesus be a fence. Do not explode onto this child. Do. Not. She has every right...

"What does he know, Nora? They gonna run out of cupcakes before long."

"I'm pregnant, Mama."

She's 30. This is not tragic. Not terrible. Never mind that Sheldon's 22-year-old daughter *also* has an *illegitimate* (that effing word) child. Never mind that in this day and age, young black women are still side-eyed for having a baby out of wedlock or being a single mother, never mind if their white husbands had hightailed off to the west or if they were the marketing director for the Charlotte Ballet. This was not tragic. Nora could do anything.

But I wish she had not turned to Tony. My God, how I wished...

I wrapped her in my arms, thinking simultaneously of all that she was about to face as a single mother (if she was, in fact, going to raise this baby), and that there was no way Food Lion was going to have decent kid-desserts left in a matter of minutes. She hugged me tightly back, then let go and said, "I'll be back in a few." And then my single, pregnant, somewhat-dishonest, apparently bisexual daughter left me standing there with approximately ten million questions.

...

Sheldon and Eddie dropped Paul off after the three of them had gone from an impromptu post-run (well, post-sleeping-in for Eddie) lunch. Jessie was still at the beach – I was proud of that girl – and most of my food prep was done. Nora did not want to talk when she got back from the store, and in spite of my heart and head in overdrive from her news, I just nodded when she said she was going back to our rental to change and get her presents and would be back in plenty of time to help me set up hors d'oeuvres.

So there I was in my "sissy's" kitchen, washing all the dishes that preparing sweet potatoes, mac and cheese, devilled eggs, beer bread dressing, and balsamic green bean salad had necessitated. Maybe I was going to spend tomorrow on the beach. Maybe I should give myself a little grace for my own emotionally-taxing year. And as I was having that thought, Jessie's fiancé walked in, took a can of actual Yoo-hoo out of the fridge, and sat at his table, smiling at me.

"You're ridiculous," I said, folding the hand towel and pondering my own beverage. Mimosas for one were no fun, but maybe a glass of wine at two in the afternoon was acceptable.

"What? Why?" He was smirking in all his Hugh-Jackman, smelly-running-clothes charm at me. He knew.

"That adorable face gets you all kinds of answers and open doors, doesn't it?" I took a moment and poured and then sat across from him.

"I find it remarkable that a recovering alcoholic has no issue being around all the wine and cocktails this family consumes," I said.

Paul shrugged. "I never considered myself a 'recovering' alcoholic. I recovered, out of fear and necessity. And out of God's grace, I don't look at the stuff the same anymore."

"Most people who quit cold turkey just trade for another addiction. So I still find you remarkable." I offered him a pretty generous smile. I only knew Paul casually before he and Jessie started, goodness, *dating* was never quite the right word. But from the first morning back in the spring when I'd found them cuddling like bunnies, he'd wormed his way into the small, soft spot of my heart. He was so dang nice and open and without pretense. And his smile was never fake, always reached his eyes. That alone coupled with his genuine worship of my girl made him tops in my book.

"Oh, but I did," he said. "For a long time, I was addicted to behaving for Leah. That got me a lack-of-divorce. I was also addicted to working for quite a few years. I think now I'm officially addicted to running. And all throughout, I've been addicted to sweet tea and sugar in general. So, you know, I have my vices. I'm not that impressive."

"I dispute that claim, sir," I said. "Anyway. You doing

okay? All the people are gonna be here before long, all their wine glasses and craziness filling up your magical cottage here."

"I can't wait," he said, and something in those smiling eyes convinced me he was being truthful. So I stayed there with him awhile, my future-brother-in-love, and we dived into our observations on a brand-new kind of Christmas, who would and wouldn't be there, how every year after this would automatically look very different, how proud we both were of Jessie for taking some quiet time that day, and whether Sheldon and I would ever move away from Charlotte, which led me to telling Paul about Nora's news before I'd even told Jessie. (Hey. Nora did not say one word about keeping it a secret. It's not like I was tagging the world in a Facebook post. Plus that no-good firefighting sperm-donor knew before me, so what difference did it even make?) Yikes. I was bitter. *Get* better, *Maggie*.

"Leah and I were always a little bit amazed that none of our daughters 'came home pregnant,'" Paul said sardonically. "With three of them, it felt like the odds were against us. And when Katy ran off to California, I figured she'd come home with twins or something."

"You sure none of them ever got pregnant?" I said. It was hallowed ground, but I knew all the tea about mine and Jessie's girls. I'm sure his had some, too.

He looked a bit taken aback. "I guess I'm not sure," he said. "It's not like they spill their guts to me about that sort of thing. I just... well, I'm grateful they all are where they are now. Even Julie seems to be in a relatively good place, considering."

He paused awkwardly at that, and after a beat, we both cracked up, as Jessie walked in.

She had a hint of sunburn on her neck and face, and I could smell the salt. Her eyes definitely showed a little post-crying-puffiness, but she looked plenty content as she took us in and smiled.

"Solving the world?" she asked, standing beside Paul and putting her hand so automatically on his shoulder. Just as naturally, he hugged it with his cheek.

"Remarking at how low our expectations have gotten after this year," he half-joked. "If we started listing the traumas and nonsense, it reads like a season of *Beverly Hills, 90210*, without the clothing budget."

Jessie and I stared at him.

"Close your mouth," Jessie told me.

"What did you just say?" I asked him.

"What did I say?" he asked back.

"*90201*? Why? Since when?" she answered for us.

Paul shrugged. "Jessie used to have it on at the office day after day. Once Kelly joined the cult and chose herself, it got a little interesting. And I noticed last week it's on Hulu, so..."

Jess and I *cracked up.* "You have officially been assimilated, Mr. Man." I got up to give them space. "I am so done. God bless you. Both of you."

I meant it lightheartedly, but when I stood eye-to-eye with her, I felt that stirring in my soul, the untold, holy, weight of everything this Christmas held. I hugged her, planning to exit swiftly and without ado and go collect my crew, but she held on and whispered,

"Tell me about Tony, okay? I'll walk you outside."

"Nope," I said, pretending my eyes weren't brimmed with tears. "Stay here and have a moment with your man. I'll be back in 60 with all of my people, and we will get this party started. And anyone who isn't here tonight doesn't have to be part of our worries, okay?"

She nodded, sending her own tears down her face with a blink. "Thanks for *all of this*, Maggie. Where would we be without you?"

"You'd be feeding seven fewer people," I answered, and took my leave, thinking of Nora and how we were really... *eight.*

[9]

"Should we sing, like the Bradys?"

Jessie smiled grandly at Summer and shook her head at her granddaughter's suggestion.

"You watch that Brady Christmas movie way too much," Sam told his daughter, mussing her hair and popping an olive in his mouth.

There was music, but it was coming from Pandora on the TV. There were definitely a lot of people. Jessie couldn't help but notice that the more obvious introverts – Travis, Nora, Sheldon and his kids, and Paul, had taken Jacob and gone to play Nintendo Switch in the Cousin Nook. The rest of them were making the best of it in all their own ways, enjoying the festive drinks and irresistible little bites of cheese and veggies and nuts Maggie has spread out everywhere, and pairing or trio-ing around the living room and kitchen, talking at reasonable volumes, except when Brittany and Summer ganged up on Katy, begging her to play some carols on her guitar. She was a dead ringer for Miranda Lambert *and* a guitar teacher, but she would not play on demand. Ever.

Already, Jessie mused to herself, she was thinking of Paul's family as her own. She missed Danielle's presence, and especially Christian and Vivi. They would see them tomorrow, but Jacob had also grown accustomed to having a cousin around his age to play with. Maya's son Quinn was barely two and not nearly as much fun (on that note and based on Quinn's brief visit, Jessie had a whole mental list of things they'd have to baby proof before Vivi was on the move).

She tried not to keep looking toward the door, waiting for David's arrival. She'd never gone more than a few weeks without seeing him, and even that was rare during his year away at USC. It had been almost five months since her baby boy (yeah, she knew…) had convinced himself he was a man and moving to Arizona with Julie was a wise investment and a big adventure. And it had been about three months since he called and said Julie was essentially kicking him out and could he come home. Thus began another roller coaster that threw her and Paul into a stalemate. He moved out. She put the house up for sale. He ended up having surgery and being homeless. Her dog died and she faced impending homelessness. It was absurd, until it all brought them together.

Except David stayed in Tennessee with his uncle and aunt and never made it back home.

"He'll be here soon, *Anne*," Altan said, slipping his arm across my shoulder, his other cradling Josie. "Here, Mama. Take her. Steady on…"

She put a hand to his face and marveled that her daughter found a man as sweet and steadfast as her daddy… and her future-stepdad, for that matter.

"We are so blessed, my son." Altan had once tried to teach

her *oğul,* a Turkish word for "son," as he called her *Anne,* Turkish for "mother." She had butchered it multiple times and terribly. Now her calling him "son" just made them both giggle. "You'd think with all these people here, I wouldn't even notice…"

She didn't bother to finish the thought, because in light of the big everything, it was so silly and meaningless. She leaned her head on his shoulder for a moment and then accepted Josie, who was awake and wearing perfect little Christmas jammies with a reindeer on the butt.

At that moment, the doorbell rang. Why would David ring the doorbell? *Because it's not his home, and he has never even been here!* Jessie answered herself. She didn't bother trying to hand Josie back to Altan. Katy had already launched herself toward the door and with nary a glance to the peephole, flung it open.

"Oh. Hi. Um, Merry Christmas. Are we expecting you?"

Jessie craned her neck to take in the young man who was decidedly not David but standing in the doorway, nonetheless. He was tall, very tall, which was accentuated by the skinniest of skinny jeans, and whoever he was, he was about to turn the heads of all the single, young females in the house with a pressed and pristine white shirt hugging his muscles and the perfectly tousled locs crowning his head.

"JAMES! Hey!" Brittney had pretty much sprinted from her post near the wine bottles to the door. She was flushed and beaming and suddenly, all things were made clear.

"Hey, babe! Sorry if I'm late." He demurely kissed her cheek, and then with an air of sophistication previously unseen in any of Brittney's *friends*, he crossed the room directly to Jessie, handed her the flat, festive box in his hand, and said, "I'd know you anywhere, Ms. Jessie. So good to meet you. Thanks for letting me crash your Christmas Eve."

Had she? Jessie smiled at him and found herself wishing

she could copy Randall's signature one-eyebrow raise toward her daughter. Instead, she peeked at the box and exclaimed, "Fannie May! Brittney has really educated you!" Their favorite chocolates from Chicagoland were a rare treat. In fact, ordering some had been on one of the many to-do-lists that Jessie hadn't gotten completed.

She would rather serve a store-bought pumpkin roll than show her surprise. It was fairly characteristic of Brit not to tell her she had a new boyfriend, much less that he was coming for their family Christmas Eve, but she'd matured a bit since Randall died, so Jessie was thrown. And James wasn't even done.

"I hope you don't mind that I brought my brother," he said. "Our dad and his wife are on a cruise until the morning, so we were going to end up at Waffle House…"

"Waffle House for Christmas is only when you've run out of options," Jessie answered. *What the hell, Brittney?* "This year, Brittney's Aunt Maggie has cooked all day for us, and it's going to be great. Maggie!"

Maggie was holding and sharing a pizzelle with Quinn. She handed him over to Abby and crossed the room, glass in hand, black curls piled atop her head and adorned with a red, green, and purple silk scarf, smile filling her whole face.

"Who's the new guy?" she asked Jessie.

"Mags, this is James. He's a friend of Brittney's, and his brother is here, too…"

They exchanged a hearty handshake while Brittney and Jessie engaged in a very silent conversation via Jessie's urgent "Why in seven hells didn't you tell me you had a boyfriend and he's coming to Christmas Eve?" squinted eyes and her "I didn't want to make a big deal" widened eyes. Altan took the opportune moment to claim his baby back and step away to the simplicity of video games.

"Oh, hello," Maggie said. When Jessie turned from

Brittney, James had been joined by a two-inch-taller version of himself, with more closely cut hair and baggier jeans, wearing just as crisp of a shirt, only in black, and a much more reserved expression on his face.

"Merry Christmas," he said, looking like he wasn't sure where he was or how he got there.

Jessie empathized. Paul had taken to calling her a closet introvert, and in that moment, she'd have much rather been on the beach alone than in her own home, filled with too many people to approximate but still holding a few distinct and sizable voids.

"Mama... Maya says Quinn needs his—oh..."

Nora had paused halfway between the doorway of the nook and where they were gathered. She was staring at James' brother with a complete lack of expression on her face. It had always been hard to tell what that child was thinking. It was even harder now that she was 30 years old.

As she walked slowly over, she asked him, "How did you know I was here?"

Clearing his throat, the young man answered, "Wow. I mean... I didn't. I don't even have your number."

"Yeah. And it is *really, really* hard to find people these days, what with personal information being so locked down on the internet and me working in marketing for a major theater in a big city..."

"It's true," added Brittney, another marketing genius in the family. "I can basically find anyone on social media if I have a mental photograph and the first two letters of their first name."

Jessie cackled in spite of herself, and was given an approving glance by Brittney, but Maggie *and* Nora were stone silent, both looking at what's-his-name.

"Well, welcome to our home, anyway," Jessie said, extending a hand. "I'm Jessie, and this is probably one of the weirdest and most chaotic holidays you'll ever attend."

"And we are just getting started," Maggie muttered.

"This is Abe," James said, catching on to the weirdness. "Abe and I are really grateful for the invite."

"There ain't no invite," Maggie said, and now I was seriously confused.

"Aunt Maggie, James and I—" Brittney started.

"Mama, please," Nora said, still looking at Abe. "You want to see the backyard with me?"

"Um, sure," Abe muttered. He looked at Jessie then, still sheepish. "Thank you for... well, thanks." He followed Nora, who was all but stomping, across the kitchen to the side door.

Jessie didn't bother with a *what in the hell?* As soon as Brittney took James by the arm to lead him to a saner side of the room, Maggie scream-whispered in her ear:

"NORA TOLD ME SHE IS PREGNANT TODAY FROM A FLING AT MY WEDDING AND I DON'T KNOW BUT I BELIEVE THAT IS THE GOD-BLESS-ED BABY DADDY!"

Baby Jesus, forgive me. Jessie's first thought was, *Thank God it's Nora and not Brittney.* Nora was older and more settled, had a better job and lived in a different town, and had a different mother so probably wouldn't need to move in with Jessie. It was big and complicated news, though. Maggie just shook her head. Jessie began for-real-whispering back all her questions, trying not to look at the clock, because two-thirds of her, at least, was still waiting on David's arrival.

"I don't think he knows," she said. "I don't think she did any light internet stalking either. It wasn't a very deeply sentimental fling, from the way it sounded."

"Shouldn't they all be raised by now?" Jessie asked, nodding a bit curtly for Christmas over in Brittney's direction. "I mean, the nerve of these kids. Mine inviting a boyfriend over here we know nothing about and yours inviting a baby and his daddy without checking first. What if we were using place cards?!"

"You're an *idiot!*" Maggie gasped, displaying Dolly Parton's favorite emotion, laughter through tears.

"You have enough food?" Jessie said, trying to calm them both.

She downed her rosé before answering. "I have enough for those two fine young cannibals and probably six more. You think Baby Boy is going to bring friends?"

The doorbell rang.

"FFS!" Jessie was whisper-screaming. "My kid isn't going to ring the doorbell, right? Is this really where we are?"

"I think that's the least of your worries," Maggie muttered.

Jessie gave her a bewildered look as she headed again to the front door, this time met by Paul.

"What is going on?" he said. "Who keeps ringing the bell?"

"It ain't all one person, Paul," Maggie called from behind them.

He rolled his eyes at Jessie. "Dinner soon?" he asked, not so much a signal that he was hungry as a signal that this was already a lot and please could they not drag this out to all hours.

"I think so." She glanced back at Maggie. "There's a little surprise drama going on, so…"

Paul was saved by the second-ringing of the doorbell. Giving Jessie's backside a quick squeeze, he kept an arm around her back as he opened the door.

She watched his face morph from casual Christmas pleasantness to mild confusion, possible foreboding. She replaced her instinctive *Who the hell?* to *Oh, holy night* and felt her stomach rage with butterflies as Paul pulled her closer, in full view of the doorway.

And there stood Jessie's brother.

And there behind him, some guy.

What? *Why?*

"Tony?" The tremble in her voice made her so angry. So angry. She wanted to feel nothing, but this season, this night, was too much for that.

"Hey sis."

Her head reeled back, and Paul was officially gaping at her. He recovered more quickly than Jessie did and muttered, "I got it." Thrusting a studied hand forward, he said, "Tony, I'm Paul. I trust my – Jessie – was not expecting you."

Dang, he's good, Jessie thought. He wasn't going to give any of their business away. He had her back. She wanted to walk through the door and just leave, with Paul.

"Hi Paul. Tony. And," Jessie's brother straightened his shoulders and looked at her, giving her a chance to notice the gray in his voluminous hair and uncharacteristic beard, the softness in his eyes, "I apologize to you both. I've heard a lot about you, Paul. Good to meet you."

"Heard from whom?" Jessie finally said. As soon as the words were out, it dawned on her, and she wondered again where in the world her baby boy was. If Tony had somehow made it, uninvited, from Arizona, surely David should have completed his six-hour trek by now.

"Never mind," she continued. "Tony, whatever this is about, it's not a good time. Not now. Maggie is here with the girls and her new husband and his family, and we are... trying to just enjoy this Christmas as much as we can..." *Since it's the first since my husband died, you horse's ass.* Paul was squeezing her hand now, and she knew he could feel her energy and her hard-fought restraint.

"Jess, I know. I know. I've been in touch with Maggie and I was going to wait until after Christmas, but Blake and I are leaving in a few days, and I didn't want to wait…"

Blake. Maggie. Maggie? Is this what she wanted to tell her? Did she know he was coming?

"Maggieeeeee!" she called, with no subtlety.

"It's almost ready!" came a bellow back from the kitchen.

"Need you out here. Now!"

The front door could be seen from almost any spot in the kitchen. Jessie was unconvinced Maggie didn't see the scuttle at the door, and she was prepared to drag her by her gold-lamé (Maggie's signature color) dress straps if she needed to.

She was trumped by Moni.

"Dad?" she said, appearing at Jessie's other side. Paul took a step back to make room for the reunion.

"Hi sweetheart."

"What are you doing here? Nora said you were coming later this week."

"Okay, but why do people know who's coming to my house and I don't?" Jessie said. She inwardly winced at the lack of sensitivity she felt toward her niece, former abandoned-child, but *hell's bells*! And who was Blake?

"Jessie, I didn't think—"

"No. You didn't. But how would you know? I mean, you had blow-by-blows from my twenty-year-old who's been gone for almost six months, so technically, you must understand everything that's going on here this Christmas. New grandbaby. Dead husband. New house. Blending families. My fiancé. All the *feels*. For God's sake, Tony. You could have *called* me! I know that's not your thing, but I didn't think crashing Christmas was either."

"Aunt Jessie, he's—"

"Oh no, darling," Jessie said, pressing her hand into her niece's hand. "Moni, I am so happy for you to catch up with your dad, but don't you dare make excuses for him. I've known him our *whole* lives. He doesn't need you to make this right for him. Everyone has time for a phone call." In Jessie's head, she heard her mother's voice, then, responding to random smelly people they'd encounter at the store or the library or even church growing up, wrinkling her nose at the "B.O." and saying, "Everyone can afford a bar of soap."

She giggled in spite of herself, or maybe because of herself. How much more ridiculous could it get? *Don't tempt fate.*

Paul was smiling as he clearly stifled his own giggle. Moni was looking at her strangely and Tony just looked uncomfortable, as he should.

"Well, y'all might as well come in," Paul said, employing a version of his principal voice again.

"Thank you." Tony stepped over the threshold and embraced Moni. Then he turned around and nodded to the lean man with floppy dark hair and tan skin behind him. He looked to be in his late 40s or so, dressed like the previous two strangers who'd graced their doorstep, with an aloof expression in his hazel eyes that Jessie might have found attractive when she was 18, but found fairly annoying on this, the Eve of their discontent. "Come on. It's fine."

Things happened in slow motion for a minute. Maggie called "Turkey's ready for carving" from the kitchen. Tony held his hand out to Blake, and when he took it, Jessie noticed there was a wedding band on each of their left ring fingers. Moni smiled at Jessie with a modicum of expectation. And then finally, Maggie was there. For the first time in Jessie's memory, she looked reproved.

"Tony," she said, nodding. *Did she sound demure? Was Jessie dreaming?*

Paul looked at Jessie with an expression echoing her thoughts. Moni smiled generously and announced, "Mama.

Aunt Jessie. Mr. Paul. This is Blake. Dad's husband."

Maybe ten, even five years or, whatever, months ago, this would have been as astonishing as her Millennial-aged niece assumed it was, but Jessie just sighed. She always figured there was some deep-seeded reason her only sibling completely abandoned his family and basically everyone he ever knew. At some point along the way, treading the deep waters of her own full life, she stopped reserving any energy for discovering or even wondering what it was.

"It's nice to meet you," Paul and Jessie said, in unison. It would have been funny any other time.

"Tony, I thought we were gonna wait on this," Maggie said. "Blake, welcome to Jessie's home, though. By all means. We are eating in just a minute."

Jessie inwardly cringed. She felt like a guest in her own home, and even more so, on a send-up of *Punk'd*.

"Thank you. And hello." Blake made eye contact with each of them, a steely resolve in his eyes. All things considered, Jessie respected that. They were all cast and characters of Tony's old life, however sad that might be. Blake was clearly his present and future and holding his own.

"Is dinner really about to start?" Tony asked. "I don't want to delay everyone."

"And yet, you showed up at 6pm on Christmas Eve? You were fixin' to delay something!"

"Mama!" Moni admonished, just as Paul said, "Maggie…"

"Honestly. Everyone. This is a lot. A *lot*," Jessie started. "Tony, Blake, Merry Christmas and all. There is plenty of food. Maggie did me a solid and cooked for two days. So stay. Enjoy your daughters. Nora is… well, Nora is out back. Maybe you should see her out there first. Just…"

"You are welcome for dinner," Paul finished for her. "Please be mindful that this is already a hard night for everyone here, and… Well, that should be enough said."

Blake nodded at Paul. Maggie was instructing her ex-husband.

"We don't have enough seats at the table as it is, so there's room out here, and there's another setting outside. It's warm enough. But Nora is out there having a discussion, so why don't you let me—"

"Why don't you let me?" Jessie said. "You get—" she gestured at Tony, "this all settled, and I will check on Nora. We need to go ahead and get this party started. I don't know what David was thinking… Tony…" *Oh, crikey. Am I really asking this guy?* "You haven't heard from him by chance, have you?"

Blake managed to look more uncomfortable as Tony stammered for an answer. "You know what?" Jessie said, sounding even to her ears like her 13-year-old self about to tick Tony off for hogging the phone. "Never mind. He'll get here when he gets here." She spared Paul a momentary soft glance before she essentially stomped to the backyard.

"Nora."

Under the beautiful old willow tree in the yard, adorned with white twinkling lights, Nora was kissing Abe. Jessie cleared her throat, and when they parted, she saw tear stains on Nora's cheeks.

"Honey, I really hate to interrupt."

"Oh my God. What now?"

Jessie figured she looked every bit as tired and exasperated as she felt. But she smiled. "I'm sorry. Everything is fine. I have no idea if this will be a surprise to you or not, but Tony is here. And he has someone with him, and they're waiting inside for you, and then they're going to stay for dinner."

"Blake."

Jessie nodded. "So you know. Okay, sister. Well, Sam is going to say grace in a minute and then we'll eat. And who knows what else? Abe, Merry Christmas, bud. I hope we are a joyous alternative to Waffle House."

She walked inside, making a beeline for Paul. Everyone was gathering into the great room, and Jacob charged her. She picked him up even though his lanky, six-year-old frame was too big for her. She squeezed him, and because he put his head on her shoulder, she covered it with kisses and let him rest there.

Altan and Mikayla were huddled together. Mikayla had tears in her eyes as she bounced up and down with Josie in her arms. Brittney had her arm through James' and was chatting with Katy. Travis, his girlfriend Cali, and Eddie stood goofing with Summer. Maggie, Sheldon, and Abby were shuffling platters across the counter. Kendall stood shyly with Quinn in her arms. And Paul put his arm around Jessie's waist and pulled her and Jacob in close as Sam cleared his throat.

"I guess we'll pray," he said. He looked up and smiled as Nora and Abe walked in from outside. Nora walked to Tony and without a verbal greeting, planted herself next to him and Blake. Almost everyone was accounted for. It was the year's theme.

"Thank you, Jesus, for Christmas," Sam began. As the bustling stopped for just a moment, Jessie peeked and saw Abby cross to her husband and take his hand. Everyone in the room was connected to someone, physically, relationally. There were people missing. There were people missed. Jessie marveled that in spite of those facts, her heart was overflowing.

"We know you've walked through this year with us, even when we couldn't see it," Sam continued. "We can look around this room tonight and know that you bring us through even the worst of times and you give us people to love." He paused, and Jessie could feel his brokenness, but she could also feel her pride. "May we be worthy. Amen."

Amen echoed in the room. Jacob unceremoniously jumped from her arms to be first to the plates. Abby started correcting him. Sam accepted Summer's teary hug. And Paul was not letting go.

"Jess," he said softly in her ear. "Merry Christmas."

She looked at him fully and openly, not afraid for him to see the conflicts and complications rising with her joy. "It is," she said, nodding, her own tears filling her eyes. "I love you, Paul."

Paul embraced her, softly answering, "I love you, Jess." And when she opened her eyes over his shoulder, she beheld another young man, with dirty blonde hair that was longer than it had been since his primary school years and hideous camo-colored Crocs on his feet, ones Jessie had sworn she'd thrown away before his initial move to campus.

David had not rung the doorbell. He smiled at her.

"Merry Christmas, Mama. I'm home."

⚝[EPILOGUE]

"**I** 'll see you next month, okay, girl?"
Jessie was holding my hand as she walked me
to the car. St. Sheldon had already been waiting
in there for like 12 extra minutes as we said our goodbyes.
We let all-the-kids drive his Lexus home and now it was
our turn, a blissful, four-hour drive ahead of us in my little
Fusion, to debrief from the 8,000 things that had happened
since we'd arrived in Surfside Beach less than a week earlier.

"I think Paul and I will come up for a visit together," Jessie
said. "I guess we need to start planning a wedding."

She was giggling, but I was grimacing. I was excited to
plan *Jessie's* wedding, but Nora's unexpected announcement
the day after Christmas felt scary and ridiculous.

"You didn't want her to be a single mother…" Jessie said.

"Please. I didn't want her to marry that guy she barely
knows, either."

"'That guy' is Abe, and you better learn his name. Our

children are *all* more stubborn than we are, and that is what should scare us far more than any one decision they make. She will not be swayed. We must stand by her."

"You sound so confident," I told her. I looked at her and tucked a stray gray strand behind her ear. "Time to go see Lexie again."

She shrugged. "Maybe I should keep the gray. Like a badge."

I shook my head. "You don't need a badge for this year, Jess. You just... you made it. You thrived. You didn't even kill your brother on Christmas Eve."

"But I wanted to," she said.

"Me too."

"Do you feel better? Forgiving him?"

"Oh Jess." We had managed not to talk about Tony – and Blake – very much since their Christmas-afternoon appearance. They saw Nora and Moni for breakfast the next day before they all, quite thankfully, left town. I assumed Jessie had her own specific feelings about my ex-husband coming out in his dramatic and typical inconsiderate fashion, but I was surprised she hadn't expressed them. She'd had more anger toward him than I did through the years.

"I forgave him a long time ago," I said. "What choice was there if I was going to be a good example to my girls? If I was going to be able to move forward with Sheldon, or anyone? But... I will say it feels nice to finally understand him. I don't agree or approve. I think he should have trusted me. I think he put the girls and me and *himself* through a lot of unnecessary wondering and hurt. But it will be better now. I believe that."

Jessie nodded, sister-warmth all over her face. "You're amazing," she said. "I still don't think he's very amazing, but I can only imagine the fear he had over being a gay man in the culture we grew up in. I can understand why he didn't want my parents to know. But he's had a lot of time to make his amends and instead—"

"Instead," I interrupted, "He got to know your baby boy and decided you had created your own culture, and it was safe for him." I kind of hated giving that man that much grace, but having needed it myself a few times, what did I have to lose now? Everything I ever had with Tony was over, save for those two amazing women he created with me.

She smiled, as she always did when David was mentioned in the context of his baby-of-the-family magic. And then she nodded, resolutely. "The least *and* the best I want for all my family is peace."

I hugged my sister tight. I still hated living far from her. Four hours seemed so far with so much happening. Nora and Abe had to figure out where they were going to live. She did want a wedding, but I wanted Jessie to have one, too. David was still going to stay in Tennessee. Brittney seemed serious with James. Everyone had a story and a drama and a thing, and it seemed the older our kids got, the older we got, Jessie and I had more things to care for, more complications.

"I always thought it would get simpler," I said aloud. I was summarizing my unspoken thoughts, but she got it.

"I think it just gets… *clearer*," she answered. "And we get stronger. And wiser. Most of the time."

"Most of the time," I repeated. Finally, I opened the car door, or else I might stay, and let myself back into her dreamhouse, and pour more coffee, and say more things.

"So, thank you for everything. *Everything.*"

"Thank you for letting me be here for you," I answered. To the extent she let me use her kitchen for Christmas, it had really been a wonder.

She smiled, sadly, gratefully. I knew if she said anything, she would cry, and I didn't want her to. So I flashed her the "I love you" sign with one hand, as the other reached for

Sheldon's, and I said the only words I had left for our visit. "Peaceful new year, Jess." And we drove.

The story continues in
RUN THE OTHER WAY

Afterword

This Hard and Holy Season

There is no 'right.' Just follow what God is putting on your heart.
Maybe in this hard and holy season, it is simply to listen and receive
and to rest. You have worked hard this year, healing and helping and
rebuilding. Maybe take 'silent night' as an invitation. Don't fix
anything. Just behold the wonders of His love.

- Carter to Jessie, Another at the Table

Remember 2020?

Haha. If you're like many of us, probably all of us, not only
will you never forget 2020, but you kinda feel like it blurred
together with 2021. Some things changed, but a lot of
things did not.

I think, though, that we forget about the *first two months* of 2020, before the word "unprecedented" made its way into our daily vocabulary, before we ever knew about that off-putting phrase that starts with "s" and ends with "distancing," before toilet paper supplies were low and anxiety for the future was at a seemingly all-time high. Remember January and February 2020? I do.

Early that year, I started a list of people we knew who had died. Yes, it's morbid I know, but even before the *pandemic*, it was a thing. It was so sad, and it looked something like this:

- the lady whom my youngest daughter befriended in our neighborhood. Kaity walked her dog every day after school and on the weekends, too. One day she went to the hospital for tests. And my baby girl never saw her again.
- a lady from my childhood church… her kids were all younger than me, but we kind of grew up together. She always sang pretty, eccentric songs. She loved her husband fiercely. She was kind of a grace hippie before it was cool, and cancer robbed her of her silver years with grown kids and grandchildren.
- a woman with whom I attended high school, who also loved *Grey's Anatomy* and *Friends* and *Beverly Hills 90210*, who became a closer friend than ever because of social media. Her husband and sons lost her so suddenly.

- a friend on Facebook only, one I'd met through a mutual friend that I don't even talk to anymore. She had a very specific ministry that spoke so intensely to my heart, focusing not only on encouraging women to seek alternative to abortion, but on assisting them in the aftermath of the decision to see through their pregnancies. In the time I knew her online, she suffered a freak accident that made the rest of her life incredibly painful *and* married her own second-chance romance. I wish I could have sat with her for just a few hours in real life.
- a young mama who suffered through her last few years battling brain tumors and the many complications they caused. Oh, how I hate when children are taken from their parents too soon (it's always too soon). But there is an unspeakable, specific heartbreak when young children lose their mama. It is so unfair.
- And finally, there was a friend, a friend of mine and the mother of my daughters' friends, who lost her boy. This precious family lost a son and brother to suicide, and it rocked our community. All the details, all the questions, all the fallout, were so tangible and so, so painful. How can you shield children from that kind of trauma? How can you rescue a mother's heart from that kind of shattering?

The answer hurts as much as the question: You *cannot*. No matter what happens next, for any of these families, there will *always* be sorrow. There will *always* be an empty seat at the table. There will *always* be people we wish they could have met, babies we wish they could have held, dreams we wish they'd witness coming true.

When I first released *The Tentative Knock,* I was afraid that I hadn't known enough grief, at least, a close enough grief, to truly express what it felt like for Jessie and Paul and their families to lose those they held most dear. And still, three years after completing the first draft of that story, I have still been protected from that level of loss. But loss is all around me, and as an empath like Jessie, I feel it in my own heart and soul. I've learned how to be comfortable sitting helplessly at someone's side and holding space for her or his grief. I have learned the difference between the time for a pep talk, the time for a prayer, and the time for abject silence. I have learned that while food and hugging and music and fellowship can be magical, there is no formula to remove sadness. The only time that will happen, I believe, is when we reach our own last days on earth, and God wipes every tear from our eyes. (Revelation 21:4)

The year 2020 went on to hold more stories of loss, unexpected, sacred. Because it was 2020, we had to shift and swerve how we did everything. That meant, through my work at our church, I became a producer of online funerals. That meant precious lives passed with no memorial service at all. That meant people died with no loved ones at their side. That meant we all ran the risk, in a year when every message from every media outlet included death, of becoming callous to what death really means.

In this hard and holy season, in the aftermath of *my* 2020, I have learned and grown. I have clung to the simple motto that *God said LIVE,* and He wants us to do so abundantly until our bodies are done. I now look back at the Christmas story in such a profoundly different way, wondering if a human father could ever do what our Heavenly Father did, allowing His Son to be born while knowing, seeing, allowing, that He would one day not only die, but suffer horribly in the process.

Like Jessie, my human heart wants to shield my loves from suffering. Oh, I believe when we die, we will be reunited with all who have gone before us and most especially with the One who made us, but there will be pain and loss and grief and hard, hard seasons during our time here. It's the consequence of living in a broken world. But aren't we wonderfully made? (Psalm 139:14). Our lives are intricate and our feelings and often our relationships *are*, yes, complicated, but I would choose that *eight-million* times over a life of simply *existing*, trying to avoid the inevitable *hard*.

Can we have the holy without the hard? I don't think we can. Before Mary and Joseph experienced their most holy night, they experienced doubt, fear, exhaustion, fear, lack, and more fear. The unknown was all they could see. Can you imagine being so young and so burdened as they were? But after a long night of labor, of suffering, of more fear, angels joined them to welcome their promise. The King had been born to them. Love had been formed in a human. A perfect baby had been born with all the promises of God and life in His tiny hands. We will all behold Him, but they got to *hold him*. Jesus came! And He came to temper the hard with the *holy*.

We are so blessed.

I pray today that you set a seat at your table for Him this year. If you have known and served the Lord in your life, hoot-nanny and Hallelujah! I hope my own love for the

Savior jumped off these pages like joy to the world. And if you're scratching your head wondering what all this has to do with the cute little romance novella you picked up or downloaded for a light Christmas read, just know that this girl right here, Kelly-from-the-Heights who found her home in the south, is simply obeying the call. God has blown my mind in 2021 with seasons of victory. I'm just following His lead and letting you know... He loves you. He will always answer the door when you knock, and there will always be a seat waiting for you at His table.

Love – and *live*,

Kelly

October 25, 2021

Acknowledgements

This story was just a snippet at the end of September 2021, when I released *The Tentative Knock*. The support of my friends and readers gave me wings. I declared my own personal "NaNoWriMo" and finished it as a Christmas gift to my early supporters, and frankly, to myself.

It is an immense thing to suddenly be living a specific dream, and I have been blessed by many along the way who helped me get here. Specifically, in this moment in time, I give my heartfelt thanks and big ol' chaotic family Christmas hugs to:

Rod Burton, the husband I was meant to have, who can talk me off any ledge, who doesn't say 'I told you so' or laugh too hard when my light bulbs finally go off, who would do anything to provide for our family, who works hard beside me, and always cheers for me. I could not ask for more or love you more.

Miranda Rose, first miracle, early reader, tiny queen. Happy 15th Birthday!

Josh, Paige, Kaity, Jack, and Kirsten and Nora, just so you don't think Miranda is my favorite. I thank you for being in my corner... I love you and our big ol' chaotic family!

Daniel McF. Brass, for turning his running store into a launch party and a pop-up bookstore. "You *are* my Ambassador of Kwan, man."

Shanilla, the voice of chosen southern sisters.

Terrie, for those magical words: "You are not alone."

Deanna and Kendall (& Paige!)... for the morning after breakfast that will ring through my life.

Marjorie, for coming through!

Mike, for responding to so many random lines and characters you can't possibly keep track of. I wish you whatever the opposite of pumpkin pie hummus is.

The running friends who turned out to be reading friends who just became *mine*: Diane (Little Sister), Dawn (Coach), Akemi (Protector), (My) Bill, Lacey (Sole Sister), Mary Claire, Jim, George, Tucker, Mylena & Brian & Team Yee, The Julies, Gypsy, Alicia, Iris, Jessica, Dr. Katie, Julia, Jen, Tracy, Kevin, and ALL of #TeamBlackDog. I am stopping because I will forget names and I don't want to...

For these people who jumped all in for me in ways I will never forget: Ed Piotrowski, Tracy, my brothers Tom, B, & Charlie, Nancy Thompson, Debbie Thurmond, Ron Fuller, Darcy, Cathy, Whitney, Cortney at The Bookworm, and Nickie Snyder.

Mom & Dad, for moving to the beach for our big, chaotic life.

To every single friend and stranger who attended that book launch, the best night ever.

To the locals who are helping me build this thing, including Megan and Surfside Library, Danyel and Patrick at WMBF, and the folks at WPDE. I love living at our beautiful beach and hope these stories honor our home!

Read all the books in the Surfside Beach series!

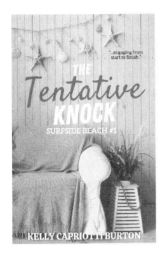 

Coming in October 2023:

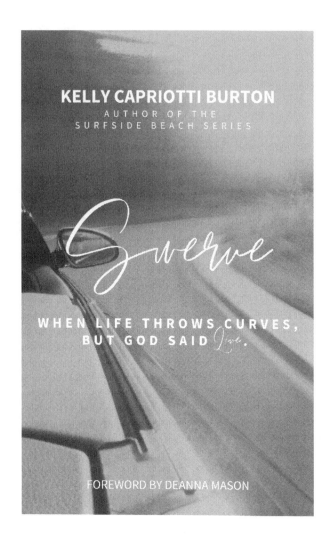

Swerve: When Life Throws Curves, But God Said Live

21 stories of messy lives & amazing grace.

NOW AVAILABLE

Made in the USA
Columbia, SC
21 March 2025